ROSE

BOOK ONE

By John McDonnell

CHAPTER ONE

June 1880. Skibbereen, Ireland.

"Have you seen him, Rose Sullivan, the fine boy looking at you all this evening?"

"Mary, how could I not?" Rose said, to her cousin Mary. "He's been staring holes in me all evening with those blazing blue eyes. Why, he's looking at me like a dog that hasn't had its dinner."

They were standing in the middle of a dirt floor in the barn of Fergus Flynn, the only person in the countryside near Skibbereen who had a barn large enough to host a proper American Wake. The place smelled of cows and horses, and it was lit by an oil lamp hanging on the wall and flickering candles placed on the rough wooden tables that had been brought in for the festivities.

The Wake was for Rose and Mary, who were leaving tomorrow morning for America.

"Then why don't you ask him to dance?" Mary said. "Old McBride is playing God's own music on the fiddle tonight, and if you don't ask the boy, I'll ask him myself. It's itching my feet are to dance."

"Wisha, what good would that do," Rose said, "with me leaving for America at break of day tomorrow? Why, we'll be on the dock at Queenstown this very time tomorrow evening."

"No better reason," Mary said, taking Rose by the arm and guiding her through the groups of dancers to the tall, black-haired boy with the sky blue eyes who was standing in the corner. "We may never come back to dear old Skibbereen, my Rose, and tonight's the night for dancing the tears away."

Rose felt a tightening in her throat at Mary's remark, and the sadness came flooding back. She had been trying not to think too much about the grim fact that she was leaving her home and family tomorrow morning and sailing to America, and that she may not ever see some of the faces in this room again.

No, she must not think of that.

Mary was right. Better to dance the night away than think of that.

She swallowed hard, looked at the boy standing in front of her, and said, "Is it your plan to stand there all night holding up the wall, or will you dance with me?"

He grinned and said, "I'm not much for dancing. It's more of a singer I am."

"You wouldn't take a spin on the floor, then?" Mary said. "It's her last night in Ireland, and the girl could use a dance to take her mind off her fate. I'm leaving myself, by the way, and if you won't dance with Rose, would you consider a spin with me?" Mary batted her eyes flirtatiously, but the black-haired boy wasn't game.

"I told you, I'm not a lad for dancing," he said. "But if you'll get your man over there to stop playing his fiddle, I'll sing you a tune."

"Maybe we don't want to hear your singing," Mary said. "Maybe we want to dance." The way she was standing with her hands on her hips, Rose knew she was spoiling for either a dance or a fight with this handsome stranger.

"Never mind, Mary," Rose said. "If it's a song he wants to sing, let's hear it." She turned to where old McBride was sawing away on the fiddle, clapped her hands, and said, "Begging your pardon, Mr. McBride, but the boyo here wants to sing."

McBride put his bow down, the dancers all stopped in their tracks, and all eyes turned to the black-haired boy, the planes of his face softened by the candlelight, who looked like an angel or perhaps a prince who'd stepped out of a dream.

He glanced around the room, smiled, and launched into "Dear Old Skibbereen", the song about the Famine of the 1840s.

> *Oh father dear, I oft-times hear*
> *You speak of Erin's isle*
> *Her lofty hills, her valleys green,*
> *Her mountains rude and wild*
> *They say she is a lovely land*
> *Wherein a saint might dwell*
> *So why did you abandon her,*
> *The reason to me tell.*

His voice was clear and pure, an achingly high tenor that took the breath away. He closed his eyes and sang with such feeling, telling the sad story of a man who had to leave his farm in Skibbereen, that before long the tears were flowing from every eye in the room.

> *Oh son, I loved my native land*
> *With energy and pride*
> *Till a blight came o'er the praties;*
> *My sheep, my cattle died*
> *My rent and taxes went unpaid,*
> *I could not them redeem*
> *And that's the cruel reason*
> *Why I left old Skibbereen.*

And when he finished with:

> *And you were only two years old*
> *And feeble was your frame*
> *I could not leave you with my friends*
> *For you bore your father's name*

I wrapped you in my cóta mór
In the dead of night unseen
I heaved a sigh and bade goodbye
To dear old Skibbereen.

There was a moment's silence and then everyone clapped and cheered. The boy broke into a grin and gave a bow to them all.

There were cries of "More! Sing another!" but he waved his hand and said, "No, let the fiddler play. It's a time for happy songs, to dance and sing, when girls like these go off on an adventure. It's starting a new life they are, and we should be celebrating."

Rose was about to urge him once more to sing another song, but all of a sudden there was a piercing wail that sent a chill through her, and she turned to see her mother, wrapped in a threadbare black shawl, her white hair askew and her eyes with a wild, unearthly light in them. She was standing in the middle of the floor, pointing a finger at Rose.

"No happy songs!" she wailed. "No jigs and reels for Rose Sullivan! My Rose, my darling Rose, she is not. The fairies took my Rose and left a foul changeling in her place. She is a fairy child, and not of my flesh."

Her voice was shrill and singsong, and it was like a knife opening a raw wound in Rose's heart once again. A wound that would not heal because her mother kept stabbing at it over and over.

Rose went over and tried to put her arm around her. "Come, mother, let us go," she said. "It's late and you are tired."

"No!" her mother said, pushing Rose so hard she knocked her to the ground. "Get away, fairy child! You are not my child! You are a fairy creature, a demon!" She made the Sign of the Cross with her bony fingers and clutched at the black crucifix hanging from her neck.

The hatred in her mother's eyes was too much to bear, and Rose felt the sadness coming back. This time she could not push it away, and she felt the tears welling up, her body racked with anguish. All the anxiety, the sadness, all the heartache came rushing back. She saw Mary and some others leading her mother out of the barn, while her mother kept screaming in her shrill voice about fairies and changelings, and then Rose felt strong arms lifting her up and helping her out the back door.

She did not realize till they were outside that the strong arms belonged to the black-haired boy.

"Come," he said. He took her hand and led her on a path that wound up a small hill, till they were standing on a rise that overlooked miles of countryside, farms and fields. It was a clear night with a huge full moon that turned the midsummer sky a deep velvet blue, and in the far distance the light of the moon spilled molten silver on the surface of the sea.

"Here," the boy said, taking his black scarf off and handing it to her. "To dry your tears."

She wiped her face and gave a long sigh. It had been hard to hold those tears back, and it was a relief to finally let them go.

There was a large flat-topped stone nearby, and the boy sat down on it and motioned for her to come over. She sat next to him and they stared out at the countryside for a time, neither one saying a word.

Finally, she said, "Forgive me for that display. Sorry I am I let myself get like that. I suppose it's because I'm leaving tomorrow. Mother is probably just having one of her spells, and she'll get over it."

"A spell is it?" he said, with a twinkle in his eye. "She wasn't telling the truth, I take it. You're not a changeling, are you?"

"She's touched in the head," Rose said, ignoring his jest. "When she was but a girl, half her family died in the Great Famine, and she was never right since. Father says people thought she was under a fairy spell, but he decided she just had a special way of looking at the world, and he fell in love with her. She can be so full of life, laughing and singing, but then a cloud will come over her face and she'll begin to wail and talk of fairies and curses. Lately, it's been getting worse."

"A crazy woman, then?"

Rose bristled. "Crazy she may be to the likes of you, but not to me. She knows so much of the old ways, the language and the lore. Why, she can tell you all about the ancient kings who lived here, the battles they fought, the beautiful queens and fierce warriors. They're all real to her, you see. She sees them as plain as if they were standing right next to her. She could have been a teacher, or a poet, in another age."

"I don't believe that all that palaver about mighty kings and queens and such like," the boy said. "It's what's kept this country down, myths and legends, misty stuff. The world is changing, exciting things are happening. We need to get that moldy nonsense out of our heads. I envy you, going to America. That's the place of the future, not Ireland. My name's Sean McCarthy, by the way. Glad to meet you."

He held out his hand and Rose took it. It was a large, strong, calloused hand, and he shook Rose's hand with force, then sat back and winked at her. It was clear he was full of himself, and confidence was not something he lacked.

"I disagree, Sean McCarthy," Rose said. "I am not going to America because it's the place of the future. I don't care a whit for that quarter of the world. I am going because my mother is daft and my father is sick and can't make enough money on the farm to pay his rent. My cousin Kate went to work in America and she sends back enough money that her family in Cork lives like royalty. She said there's jobs aplenty there, working for the rich people, if only a girl will put her nose to it and work hard."

"So you'll be a servant girl for the rich, will you?"

"I'll do whatever it takes to keep my family from the workhouse. I'm the eldest girl. There's only my lazy brother Brian and my two younger sisters, Theresa and Annie, so it's up to me to do something to save this family. I intend to work hard for ten years and then come back."

"Ah, but then you'll be a dried up old biddy," Sean said. "Sure, and you're a young girl with the whole wide world in front of you. Why do you want to go to a place like America and spend all your time trying to get back here? Why, there's excitement and promise there, they say, and if it was me I'd be enjoying it to the full, with no thought of coming back."

"I owe it to my family," Rose said. "Wouldn't you do the same for yours?"

He frowned. "Maybe if I had a family, my girl, but I don't. My mother died when I was only six, and my father left soon after. He was not a man to be bothered with families. I've been fending for myself for ten years now, and I have no ties to family or village or country. I'm like a wild horse, living wherever I please."

"I feel sorry for you then," Rose said. "Family is everything to me."

"Is it?" Sean said. "Then why are you leaving them?"

Rose wanted to slap him for his impudence, but she knew he was partly right. Why was she leaving? Was it really to save her family she was going to America? Or was it because she secretly did long for the excitement, the freshness, of a new start? In her times of madness Rose's mother often spoke about a curse on the family, and sometimes Rose thought she was right, that there was a curse, and it was best to just leave this spirit haunted land and be done with it. She could never admit that, though.

"I told you before, I'm leaving only to make enough money to help my family," she said. "And then it's back I'll come. I'm only 16, and I'll still be in the flower of youth when I get back."

"Why, you're the same age as me," Sean said. "It's a glorious time to be young isn't it? Look at that sea out there. Doesn't it stir your heart and make you glad to be alive?"

Rose looked out at the moon-washed silvery waves miles away. There was something about this boy that made her smile. He seemed so carefree and spirited and ready for fun, and the sadness of her mother's condition lifted from her like a cloud passing across the face of the moon.

"There's a big world beyond that sea, and adventures to be had," Sean said. "Doesn't it make you excited just to think of it? Cross that sea and you can be anyone you want!"

"It's nonsense you're talking," Rose said. "I'll still be Rose Sullivan from Skibbereen, no matter where I go."

"No, you'll be different, my girl," Sean said. "If you go over there, it's natural to change. That's why it will be hard to come back: You'll not be the same person you were when you left. Everything changes, nothing stays the same. But that's the beauty of it! Don't you long for something different than this life? Scraping along on the edge of the sea like this, on your little square of land, living the same life your family lived for generations?"

God help her, but she did thrill to the message in his words. She did sometimes long for something different, something entirely different, than this life. What it was she did not know. Was that why her mother called her a changeling? Because she was not content with the life she had here in Skibbereen?

When Rose was a little girl her mother had often told stories about the pooka, the demon horse of legend, that had been known to carry people off, never to be seen again. The story always frightened Rose, and she would lie in her bed and sometimes think she heard the ringing of a horse's hooves on the stone path outside her window. Along with the fright was curiosity, though. She sometimes wondered what it would be like to ride on the back of a snorting black horse, galloping along a moonlit road to a rendezvous with the timeless beings that lived at the tops of hills and inside the ancient mounds.

But that was not something to tell Sean McCarthy, was it?

Just then something caught Rose's eye. It was a shooting star, in the dark quarter of the sky toward the horizon. It came and went so fast that she hardly knew what it was.

"Did you see that?" Sean said. "'Twas a shooting star. Now, that's a sign of good luck, is it not?"

And he leaned over and kissed her, full on the mouth. Rose was so startled she didn't know what to do at first, but his lips were so insistent that she found herself kissing back. It was the first time she'd been kissed like that, but Sean seemed very confident, as if he'd had lots of practice. His lips were soft and pliant, sending a charge through her body like a lightning bolt. Her breath came in shallow gasps, and her skin was on fire. A hunger inside her awoke, and it was something she didn't know had been there before.

He pulled her close, and his fingers ran through her long hair, then brushed against her cheek. His touch was surprisingly gentle, despite his calloused hands. She felt herself being swept along, panting for breath, like the time as a child when she'd been caught in a river current and got swept along until she managed to grab a tree root in the riverbank and pull herself to safety.

She pushed him away.

"Wh-what are you doing?" she said, struggling for breath.

"Begging your pardon," Sean said. "Sorry to startle you like that. It's just, don't you know it's good luck for a man to kiss a pretty girl when he sees a shooting star?"

"I ought to slap you, you brazen fellow," Rose said. Her face was flushed, her heart was racing, and she could hardly speak for panting, but she wanted him to know he couldn't do a thing like that to Rose Sullivan.

"I told you I'm sorry," Sean said. He stood up and swept his arm toward the sky. "It's just, that vision out there makes me lose my head. I get so filled up with the beauty and magic of Life that I could burst sometimes. I go daft, I guess. You're such a pretty girl, and there may never be another night like this, and I just got carried away. But don't you feel it, Rose? You're going away, leaving your home, everything you know and love. It's frightening, but damned exciting, too. Doesn't it just fill you with awe? Why, it's a special night, and I think a kiss is not a bad thing under the circumstances."

"Wisha, listen to the blarney coming from your lips," Rose said. "It's not the night or the shooting stars that have got ahold of you, Sean McCarthy. It's something else entirely, and don't try to tell me different."

"Well, I'll not deny I fell under the influence of your beauty," he said, winking at her.

"Enough," Rose said, standing up. "I'd best be getting back to my own party. They'll be out looking for me before long, and my father won't be happy to see me alone up here with the likes of you."

"Will you remember me, Rose Sullivan?" Sean said. "Will you remember me when you're far away in America? Tell me you will."

"Aye, to be sure I'll remember you," Rose said, starting down the path toward the barn. "How could I forget such a bold young article as yourself?"

"Don't be surprised if you see me there after a time," Sean said. "I have grand big dreams, and they can't be realized in this old, tired country. I need to go to a place where people do grand things."

"Then good luck to you," Rose said. "But you won't see me there for long. America to me is nothing but a place to make money, that's all. I'll be back in ten years."

"Don't be so sure," Sean said. "There's many who go over there and never come back. Look around you, Rose. The villages are emptying out, the farms lie fallow. Ireland is losing all its young people since the time of the Famine. There's no future here for them. The future is across the sea, my girl."

They were closer to the barn now, and the lively music from old McBride's fiddle came spilling out into the night air as someone opened a door. They could hear clapping and singing and happy voices.

"Listen to that, Sean McCarthy," Rose said. "That's the sound of my soul. That's my people, the very roots of me. I can no more leave it forever than I can cut off my right arm. I will be back, I promise you."

"Then glad I am that I stole that kiss," Sean said, "for I may never see you again, and at least I'll have the memory of that kiss to keep inside forever. Goodbye, Rose Sullivan."

And he turned and walked away into the night.

CHAPTER TWO

"Oh, Rose, I wish I'd never set foot on this ship," Mary moaned. She was curled up in a hammock directly above Rose, and she had been making a terrible racket, complaining mightily about her queasy stomach ever since the storm started several hours ago. Rose herself wasn't feeling much better, having already made two trips up on deck to vomit over the side of the ship as it pitched and rolled in the storm's fury.

"Don't think of it, Mary," Rose said. "Sure and it'll blow itself out after a time. Say your prayers, and it'll take your mind off the situation."

"It's saying my prayers I've been doing this whole blessed night," Mary said, groaning. "And my mind hasn't stopped. It's telling me we made a mistake leaving Ireland, and we're going to perish before we ever get to America. God is punishing us for our hunger for money."

"Now you're talking nonsense," Rose said. "God wouldn't punish us for trying to help our families. We're just trying to do our best for the people we love, and what's the wrong in that?"

Just then the ship shuddered and plunged down a great wave, and the hammocks swung against the walls while the belongings of the people around them belowdecks crashed and there were moans and cries of, "God save us!" from every quarter. The storm had come on them just after sunset, and it had been thrashing the ship about for what seemed like an eternity. Not only that, but the ship groaned and creaked with every buffet, as if it were about to splinter apart with each wave.

"If I ever get off this ship I'll kiss the ground and never leave it again," Mary said, as the ship settled itself before the next wave. "I'll never get on another one of these floating coffins as long as I live."

"Sure, and you'd never see Ireland again if you did that," Rose said. "Unless you know another way of getting home, you'll have to take a ship to come back."

"God help me, if I have to take a ship I'll never see my home again," Mary said, as another boom of thunder roared in the background.

"Now, Mary, don't talk such nonsense," Rose said. "We'll all be going home again, God willing."

"We should have stayed," Mary said. "If I was you, Rose Sullivan, I'd never have left, not with that fine McCarthy boy making eyes at me like he did to you."

"He did more than that," Rose said, mischievously. She was trying to distract the two of them from the terrible storm, and she thought talk of Sean McCarthy might do that.

"What do you mean?" Mary said.

"Why, he kissed me, don't you know," Rose said, feeling the color rise to her cheeks.

"Kissed you?" Mary poked her head out of her covers, and looked down at Rose. "Why the devil didn't you tell me this before? That black-haired boy kissed you? What was it like, Rose? Tell me this instant."

"It was like a spark of fire on my lips, and it spread through my whole body," Rose said. "I can tell you it kept me warm the rest of the night."

"You don't say! How many times?"

"Just once! What kind of a girl do you think I am, Mary Driscoll? Do you think I'd be kissing a strange boy the whole night through?"

"No, but I can tell you what I'd have done," Mary said. "I'd have sold my ticket on this blasted ship, and home I'd stay if a boy who looked like that kissed me."

For the twentieth time in the last couple of days Rose wondered the same thing. The very thought of Sean McCarthy's kiss made her heart pound and her breath come short. Strange new feelings welled up in her, and she could hardly think straight. Should she have stayed home, abandoned her plans to go to America and save her family?

One look at the miserable conditions around her was enough to quell those thoughts. Everywhere she turned there were ragtag Irish, dressed in tattered clothes and clutching their few possessions close to them, moaning in misery in the dank, smelly bowels of the ship. Desperation shone in their eyes, and a hunger for something better. They had been pushed to this point by a country that had nothing left for them, no hope of anything save a life of poverty on land that was not their own, in a world that could find no use for them.

She thought of her own family, her damaged mother wandering the fields talking to herself about "The Good People", the fairy folk, whose name must never be mentioned, her poor father whose body was stiff with rheumatism, her brother who was already turning bitter at 18 about his prospects in this hard land, and her two younger sisters whose bodies were thin and whose faces were hollow with hunger.

It was up to her, Rose, to do something about it. She had long assumed the role of caretaker in the family, doing the chores and the nurturing that her mother had abandoned. She was "little mother", as her father Abraham had called her since she was a young girl. She could not abandon that role to run after a handsome boy with tender lips. She must do her job, do what was expected of her, no matter how hard. It was up to her to save the family.

"Ah, it wasn't meant to be," Rose said. "I have a task to carry out, and I can't let my head be turned by one kiss from a handsome boyo."

"Rose, you're a better girl than me," Mary said, as the ship shuddered and groaned and rolled down another wave. "I'd give anything to be back in Skibbereen right now, sporting around with a boy like Sean McCarthy."

"Now, Mary, think of the wonders we'll see in America," Rose said. "Besides, there'll be plenty of handsome boys there, I'm sure. Doesn't your sister Kate say so in her letters?"

"That she does," Mary said, warming to the subject. "She says they have dances there that all the folks from home goes to. She says the girls get all dressed up in their finest clothes, and they have the money to buy the latest fashions, you know. She sent us a picture of herself in a dress with buttons all the way up the front, and a fancy hat, and looking like the Queen herself she was. She says everybody has money in America. The people she works for have a big house with fine furniture and silver forks and spoons, and they eat steak and kidney pie every night for dinner. They have a fine carriage with handsome horses, and they dress in the latest fashions from Paris."

"And she says there's work for us?" Rose said. "She can get us jobs in such a grand place?"

"To be sure," Mary said. "Kate says they need more serving girls, and she told them we're two respectable girls who'll be arriving soon. We'll be living the high life yet, Rose Sullivan." She groaned as the ship lurched again and the thunder boomed. "If only we make it across this terrible ocean in the first place."

They did make it across, much to Mary's relief, and she did kiss the ground as soon as she came down the gangplank. They were in Philadelphia, and a crowded, busy city it was, with more people than they had ever seen in their little town of Skibbereen. The scene at the dock was pure chaos, with people shouting for their relatives and friends, police bellowing orders, children crying, Irish runners strong-arming the new emigrants with offers of a room or a job for a price, and everything a whirl of noise and activity.

In the middle of all this pandemonium there suddenly came a terrible clanging noise and a horse standing only yards away from Rose reared up and threw its rider, a mounted policeman.

People screamed and backed away, while the horse went racing about, its eyes wide in terror, the smell of its animal fear blanketing the air. Suddenly there appeared something that looked like a red and black train car, running along tracks in the street and connected to wires overhead. There were sparks coming from the wires and a burning, acrid smell everywhere. There was a driver visible in the front window, in a blue uniform and cap. He was waving his hands frantically, and Rose saw with horror what he was looking at.

There was an old Irish man directly in front of the car. He was sitting on a large brown steamer trunk that he had put down on the track -- probably looking for a spot to rest after the long sea journey -- and he was frozen in terror, incapable of moving in time to get out of the way of the terrible contraption that was bearing down on him.

"Move!" a policeman cried. "Get off the tracks!" but the old man just sat there, his eyes as wide as saucers, an unlit clay pipe sticking out from between his teeth.

Someone in the crowd screamed, and Rose put her hands to her face, expecting the old man to be run over any second, but then, just before the moment of impact a young policeman ran over, dove headfirst into the man, and the two of them went sprawling onto the cobblestoned street next to the tracks. The train car collided with the steamer trunk and its top popped open, spilling its contents everywhere, along with the remnants of the trunk itself.

A large police sergeant ran over to the old man, and said, "What the devil do you mean, sitting down on a streetcar track?" His face was red with anger, and he was shaking his billy club at the old man. "You almost killed Officer Brooks over there, and you could have been killed yourself."

The old man had tears running down his face, as he surveyed the wreckage of his trunk. "Begging your pardon, Your Honor, but that's all the possessions I have in the world. I didn't want to lose them. I never seen such a thing as that machine coming at me, and I froze."

"Stupid Irish," the policeman said. "God help me, dealing with the likes of you potato farmers."

"Aye, he's a farmer," Mary said, her dander up. "And he's never seen a contraption like that in the fields of Ireland." She went over and helped the man to his feet while continuing her harangue. "You should be ashamed of yourself, too, belittling a poor old man like this for being afraid of something he's never seen before."

Mary's wrath was something to see, and the policeman seemed stunned by it. "Well, he'd better get used to it," he stammered. "It's called a streetcar, and we have a lot of them in America."

"And a foul noisy thing it is," Mary said.

"But it's the latest thing," the policeman said, backing away as Mary came closer to him. "It's Progress."

"Progress isn't worth a man's life," Mary said. "Now, you help me pick up this poor man's belongings, before another one of them mechanical marvels comes along."

Rose had to laugh at Mary's brazenness, ordering a policeman about like that. There was something about her that struck fear in the hearts of men, to be sure, and the policeman quickly helped her gather up the man's clothes and possessions and he even located an old packing crate and helped her put everything in that.

When they were finished, Rose and Mary helped the man find his sister, who was searching for him among the crowd of people at the dock. Once the old man was safely reunited with his kin, the girls went on their way.

Mary's sister had sent them money and instructions to stay at a boarding house a few blocks from the dock, "where the proprietor is honest and won't rob you blind," and they found a room at the top floor of a crowded brick house. They shared it with an old woman from Cork and her daughter, both of whom spoke only Irish. Rose wondered how the two women would make their way in this new land when they didn't speak the language, but she didn't have time to find out. She and Mary had to say goodbye the next day when they boarded a train for Pittsburgh, where Mary's sister Kate was going to get them jobs.

They sat in wonderment at the passing landscape that was so varied, with mountains higher and valleys lower than any they'd seen in County Cork. There were fields of wheat and corn that stretched for miles, and there were towns and villages bustling with activity and commerce. The voices of the people sounded strange to their ears, with a nasal whine, and a flat Saxon abruptness to the words that was different from the lilt of their native land. Rose missed her family already, and she wondered what they were doing this very moment, whether they were sitting around the turf fire in the cottage thinking of her, wondering about her adventures in crossing the great ocean, or whether they had started to forget her?

And what of Sean McCarthy? Had he forgotten her the moment he walked down that path and left?

"Remember me, Rose Sullivan," he'd said. That would be no problem for her; she could hardly keep him out of her mind. The black hair and blue eyes, the sound of his high, clear, tenor voice. The taste of his lips. Ah, but she couldn't let her mind go in that direction. Sure it was that she would never see him again. How could she? She could tell already that this land was too big, too crowded with people, for Sean McCarthy to find her.

If he ever came over in the first place.

She realized she knew nothing of him, not a bit. He had not spoken of his family, or where he was from. There were McCarthys living in County Cork -- their clan went back many generations -- but he had never said if he was related to them. He was a mystery man, that was sure.

"Rose, you're off in one of your dreams again," Mary said, poking her in the ribs. "You've been very distracted these days. Are you thinking of Sean McCarthy?"

"Now why would you think that?" Rose said, although she could feel herself blushing with embarrassment. "Oh, all right. I have been thinking of the boyo, but I don't know why. It'll be a miracle if ever I see him again."

"And are you a prophetess, then?" Mary said. "None of us can see into the future, Rose. You don't know if that boy will show up in your life again, just as we don't know what's waiting for us in Pittsburgh. Trust in God, girl, everything will turn out all right."

"Mary, it does me good to hear you say that," Rose said. "I don't know what I'd do without you to buck me up at times like this."

"That's my job," Mary said, smiling. "And you'll do the same for me. Let's promise that no matter what happens to us in America, we'll always be there for each other." She took Rose's hand. "Promise?"

"Promise," Rose said.

CHAPTER THREE

From the time the train pulled in to the station at Pittsburgh and Mary's sister Kate met them on the platform, things went by in a blur for Rose. There was so much to see and learn and do that she felt sometimes like her head would burst from taking it all in.

Their employer was Mr. John Overton, a brusque, no-nonsense man who worked for the railroad and had financial interests in several other businesses, including a natural gas well. His wife was Nancy Overton, a tall, thin-lipped, haughty woman who ran her household with a firm hand. They had four daughters: Melissa, Victoria, Jane, and baby Caroline. Melissa was the oldest, at 15, while Victoria was 12 and Jane was 10. Caroline was 5.

They lived in a mansion on a hill overlooking the Monongahela river and the tall buildings and blast furnaces of Pittsburgh. Rose had never been in a house so big, and its many rooms and gables and peaked roofs were confusing and disorienting.

"How do you find your way around here?" she said to Kate. "I'd be lost forever in all these rooms and passageways."

"Oh, it's not that bad," Kate said. "You'll get used to it, Rose. And all the traipsing up and down steps will keep you fit."

"It hasn't kept her fit," Mary said, when they were alone in the attic bedroom that Kate had said was theirs, and they were unpacking their steamer trunks. "Why, I'm sure she wasn't that stout when she left Ireland. I'm thinking she's eating a sight better here."

"And what's wrong with that?" Rose said. "None of us had enough to eat back in Cork. My two sisters look like skeletons. It's the reason I came here, to send money back and put some meat on their bones."

"Well, you'll have your chance," Mary said. "Mrs. Overton said we're to be paid four dollars a week! Faith, I feel rich already. I don't know what I'll do with all that money."

"You'll be smart to put some of it away and send the rest back home," Rose said. "That's what I'll be doing."

"Ah, Kate sends enough home to feed the lot of them," Mary said. "I'll do my share, but I'm not going to live like a nun. Did you see some of the clothes on the women over here? I picked out two or three dresses and hats already that I'd like for myself. I'll be the finest-looking serving girl in Pittsburgh, I will."

"And you'll be the stupidest," Rose said. "Spending your money on silks and satins! That's no way for a good Irish girl to live."

"It is if she wants to meet a man," Mary said. "I like this place already, Rose Sullivan, and I've no intention of going back to that miserable farm in Cork. I want a better life. I'll meet a man here and marry him, and I'll have the life I long for."

"Why Mary," Rose said. "I'm shocked at you. I thought you were only here to help the people at home, like I am."

"It's no life back there," Mary said. "Look around you, Rose. They have trains that run on the road here, and gas lamps on the street, and a stove that's run with gas instead of a miserable peat fire like we had at home. They have brass handles on the doors, and steak on the table at night, and fine clothes to wear. The whole place gives off an air of progress, of invention, of excitement. It's where I want to be, and I'll make a life here no matter what."

"Then God be with you, Mary," Rose said, "but I won't be sharing your dream. It's back to Ireland for me, in ten years' time."

As time went on Rose never lost her determination to go back. There was a lot to learn, though, and she barely had time to think of Ireland from morning till night. She and Mary were up at dawn to make the breakfast for the family, then they had to clean up, make the beds, sweep out the rooms and the downstairs, polish the silverware and the furniture, dust the whole house, go to the market and buy food for dinner, make the luncheon and the dinner, then clean up after that. Two days a week they had laundry to do, plus ironing, and many other tasks that left Rose weary and ready to fall in bed at night and sleep soundly till it was time to get up and do it all over again the next day.

Mary's sister Kate had a little bit of education, so she had responsibility for the girls, tutoring them in French and Latin, making sure they practiced their violin and piano, taking them in the carriage to their dance lessons, among other things. It was an easier life, but she had earned it -- she had started ten years ago doing the very work Rose and Mary did, and she had worked her way up to a nanny position. Kate was lame, from an accident in her youth, and she walked with a limp, so it was a good thing that she had advanced to an easier station. She liked the Overton girls and they were obviously fond of her, calling her "Aunty Kate".

At night she would sometimes come up to Mary and Rose's cramped attic bedroom and gossip with them, tipping them off to all the personalities of the household. She told them in a whisper that they had to beware of Mr. Overton, who often developed a fondness for the serving girls, and sometimes tried to kiss them if he caught them alone.

"It's the reason they can't keep girls here," Kate said. "Since I've been here it's been a revolving door -- girls are always quitting or getting fired because of Mr. Overton."

"Then how have you lasted this long?" Mary said. "Hasn't he tried something with you?"

"You see this foot, don't you?" Kate said. "He won't try anything because I'm damaged, in a manner of speaking. The mistress knows that, and it's why she trusts me around him. Two pretty young things like yourselves, though -- that'll be a different story."

"I'll keep my eye out for him then," Mary said. "And it's sorry he'll be if he ever lays a hand on me. I'll crown him with a frying pan, I will."

"And you'll regret that to your dying day," Kate said. "Don't you know that he's a rich and powerful man, and he could make sure you don't get another place in Pittsburgh if ever you tried something like that? There's nobody would hire you with a black mark like that on your record. Worse, he could have you on the next boat back to Ireland quick as a flash.

"No," she continued, "you girls just stay close to me, and I'll make sure nothing happens. I can handle the old reprobate."

Rose kept a watchful eye around Mr. Overton, who was a large, ruddy complexioned man with an auburn mustache. He was a man of action, who was often out of the house looking after his business interests, and for many months Rose saw little of him.

However, Mr. Overton took a liking to Rose, calling her, "red-haired Rosie" and teasing her mercilessly when he was around, and it wasn't long before the lady of the house noticed.

One morning when Rose was serving tea to Mrs. Overton in the parlor, she said, "Have you ever been kissed, Rose?"

"Beg your pardon, ma'am?" Rose said, feeling herself blush deep red.

"Oh, don't be so shy," Mrs. Overton said. "A pretty girl like you must have been kissed by now. Tell me, has a boy ever kissed you?"

Rose found herself thinking once again of the shockingly powerful kiss of Sean McCarthy. "Well, ah, I suppose I have, ma'am."

Mrs. Overton sipped her tea and smiled. "You suppose you have? I would think you wouldn't have to suppose about something like that. Have you been kissed or not?"

"I have, ma'am," Rose said. "By a boy at home."

"And what was it like?"

"It was very nice," Rose said.

"Nice," Mrs. Overton said. She took a sip of tea and pondered that answer. She smiled again. "I'm sure it was more than nice, from the way your face has turned scarlet. Be that as it may, I'm glad that you have had the pleasure of being kissed already, because then you will not make the mistake that some other girls have made in this house."

"Ma'am?" Rose said. "I don't understand."

"What I am saying is that in the course of working here you may be subject to some, ah, attentions from Mr. Overton," she said. "He is a bold, active man, and he is used to seizing the opportunity, as he calls it, in business. This quality of forceful action is an asset for a businessman, but not for a husband and father." She looked out the window, and Rose detected a great sadness in her eyes.

"There are times when he, ah. . . well, he gives in to his carnal impulses and takes liberties with. . . ah, the domestic staff."

"Begging your pardon, ma'am," Rose said. "I still don't understand."

"You can't be that stupid," Mrs. Overton snapped. "I will speak plainly: He will do what that boy in your home town did, what all men do." She put the teacup down with a clatter. "But I daresay he will be more forceful about it than your country swain."

Rose looked down in silence.

"I am warning you," Mrs. Overton said, an angry edge to her voice. "If this happens, you will be dismissed immediately. I cannot have my serving girls seducing my husband."

"Seducing, ma'am?" Rose said. "But I would never--"

"Silence!" the lady said, her eyes blazing. "Do not talk back to me. I have long and bitter experience with these situations, and I know how they happen. I am only telling you this so that you know what to expect. And so that you have no illusions about his feelings for you. Certain girls in the past have had the foolish idea that my husband was in love with them. I suppose it is natural for a simple Irish girl who's never been kissed by a man like John Overton to think such a thing, but the fact is he will never leave me for the likes of you, and the sooner you understand that the better." She was gripping the arms of her chair with such force that her knuckles were turning white.

"Yes, ma'am," Rose said. She felt the blood rise to her face again, and she fought to control her anger at this casual insult.

"Good," Mrs. Overton said. Rose suddenly felt sorry for her, because Mrs. Overton seemed humiliated by the whole conversation, and she was relieved when the lady ended the awkwardness by saying, "You may go."

After that Rose was even more wary around Mr. Overton, and as the months went by she thought that perhaps her vigilance had paid off. He had been away on business quite a lot, and when he was in the house he seemed to be ignoring her.

Then one day it happened.

He came up behind her when she was in the kitchen scrubbing a large black pot that had been used to make soup, and she was so intent on her work that she was unaware of his presence until she felt a hand on her shoulder. She turned to see who had touched her and all of a sudden his lips were on her mouth and he was pressing her back against the sink.

He was a bull of a man and he pinned her with his body so that she could neither move nor cry out. One hand cupped her behind the head while the other roamed along her skirt. His stiff mustache brushed against her cheek like the wire bristles of a brush and his tongue tried to force its way into her mouth. She could hardly breathe; he was suffocating her with his brute force.

She reached around behind her and her fingers closed around the neck of an empty wine decanter in the cast iron sink. She realized she could bring it around swiftly and break it over his head, and she gathered herself for the blow.

Suddenly, there was a voice: "Why, Mr. Overton, I'm shocked! Is that young Rose you're kissing?"

It was Kate.

Immediately Overton released his grip and backed away. He was breathing hard, trying to collect himself, and his face was flushed. He looked at Kate, who was standing at the door to the kitchen, and it was clear he would have liked to strangle her. However, with a great effort he mastered himself, and a smile flickered on his lips.

"My dear Kate, it seems you have caught me in the midst of a moment's passion," he said. "I find myself entranced by the beauty of our red-haired Rosie, and, well, I am only a man after all, subject to the sweet presence of such a lovely creature in my house. When a girl like Rosie smiles and winks at me, it is a powerful seduction. You would not understand, I am sure, but I pray you will not tell Mrs. Overton of my indiscretion."

"I understand, Mr. Overton," Kate said. "I will not trouble the mistress with this. Of course, I would be very surprised to ever see it happen again, sir."

Overton burst out in a braying laugh. "That is a matter you'll have to take up with our sweet Rosie here. When she gives me that come-hither look I confess I can't quite control myself. Well, excuse me, I must be going."

He turned and winked at Rose, and then he saw the wine decanter in her hand. All at once his face registered the fact that Rose had been ready to hit him with the heavy glass bottle. Anger flashed from his eyes, and then something else, something colder. Revenge.

For just a moment, he looked like he was ready to come over and slap the bottle out of Rose's grip and then put his thick hands on her neck and throttle her. Then, just as quickly, he mastered himself. He turned on his heel and walked out, and when he did Rose dropped the bottle in the sink with a clatter and burst into tears.

Kate came over and held her close, stroking her hair and murmuring to her. "There, there," she said. "Don't worry about it, Rose dear."

"But he's lying," Rose said, through her sobs. "I never did or said a thing to him to make him think that I would. . ."

"Don't bother yourself about it," Kate said. "He's like that with all the girls. Blames everything on them, he does. He can't be trusted. I'll have to look after you more closely now. I should never have let you out of my sight in the first place. It's all right, dear, don't cry."

I could have killed him, Rose thought. She looked down at the heavy glass bottle in the sink, the light reflecting off its many facets, and realized how quickly her future could have been changed. One blow from that decanter and Overton would have at the least received a serious cut to the head, and he'd have been bleeding like a stuck pig.

She'd have been dismissed from service, and probably sent back to Ireland, with no prospects of coming back, and no chance to make money for her family.

All her dreams could have ended in one instant.

She was shaking with terror, and it took a long time for Kate to calm her down. That night at dinner Mr. Overton ignored her completely, almost as if she were invisible. His daughters chattered away, telling their mother about the adventures they had earlier when Kate had taken them into the city to a museum, but there was a coldness around Mr. Overton, and he spent long minutes simply staring into his wine glass.

"I'd have killed the brute," Mary said that night when they were back in their bedroom. "I'd have hit him with the bottle even after Kate came in. I'd have made sure he didn't try that again with me."

"And you'd have lost your job," Rose said. "Did you not hear what Kate said about him? It's always the girls who suffer when he does these things. The mistress as much as told me that if something happens it'll be myself who gets the blame. I can't afford to be sent back, Mary. My family is depending on me."

"Ah, they'll survive," Mary said. "Haven't they got along all this time? There have been Sullivans in County Cork for ages past, and they'll be there for ages to come. They can't be killed off, my girl."

But Rose was not convinced. She fell asleep with a sense of unease, as if something bad was about to happen, and she had strange, restless dreams all night long.

The next morning, after the breakfast had been cleared away, and Mr. Overton had left for the day, Mrs. Overton called her in to the parlor.

"Sit down, Rose," she said.

Rose took a seat on a sofa across from the lady. She was rarely invited to sit in the parlor, and her heart was pounding as she looked at the stony face across from her.

"Rose, my husband has told me that you tried to seduce him yesterday in the kitchen. I cannot have this type of immoral behavior in my home. I am dismissing you at once, and I suggest that you make plans to return to your homeland. I will not give you a reference for another job in service."

CHAPTER FOUR

May 1882

Philadelphia, PA

Dear Mum and Da, Brian, Theresa and Annie,

I am sorry I have not written in so long. There have been many times when I wanted to write you a letter, but I have been so busy that I can barely keep my eyes open when I get back to my room at night, and if I sit on my bed to write, before I know it I am sound asleep.

Then too, I wanted to wait until I could send you some money. I could not do it before now, because I lost my position in Pittsburgh some time ago, and it took many months to get situated in a new one.

It is a long story about what happened in Pittsburgh, but you can be sure that I did nothing morally wrong, Father. I would never bring shame upon our family. I was a victim of an unjust employer, and I was wrongfully discharged. The woman of the house would not give me a good reference, and at first I thought I would never be able to work in America again. Cousin Mary thought this situation so unjust that she quit their employ on the spot.

It was a tragic circumstance we found ourselves in, and I thought all was lost. I was so sad, but dear Kate saved the day for Mary and me, and for that I am eternally grateful.

Kate knows the owner of an agency in Philadelphia that places Irish girls in domestic service. She packed us off on the train to Philadelphia and gave us a letter explaining the sad story. The owner, a Mrs. Brown, was sympathetic, because she has seen this same thing happen to other girls. The employers know they have the advantage over us, and some of them use that in despicable ways.

Mrs. Brown offered us lodging in her house while she looked for positions for us. It took some time, but finally she was able to find work for both of us with a family in Chestnut Hill, a town on the outskirts of Philadelphia.

The family name is Lancaster, and it has been a blessing to work for them. They have a large stone house here with many rooms, and Mary says we live like royalty. Mr. Lancaster works for the Pennsylvania Railroad, and he is a dignified man who has a position of some importance. Mrs. Lancaster is a fine, tall Protestant woman and she has been kind to me. They have a son named Martin who is 18, a daughter named Victoria who is 14, and the youngest child is Tom, who is six years old.

I receive five dollars a week in wages, more than I got in Pittsburgh, and I save most of it, unlike Mary, who spends most of her pay on fine clothes. I saved up sixty dollars, and I am enclosing it in this letter. I hope it will help you to pay the rent on the farm for some months, and that the girls and Brian will have enough to eat, and perhaps you can buy a few more pigs to fatten up and sell at the market when they are grown. I will send more money when I can.

The mistress seems happy with us here, and has no complaints about our work. There was so much to learn, but I had the advantage that I already knew a lot from working for Mrs. Overton in Pittsburgh. Mary and I are kept busy from morning till night with cleaning, cooking, laundry, polishing, waxing and all the other duties that go into keeping a house like this running.

I have Sunday and Thursday afternoons off, and I look forward to those times to get out and see others of my kind. On Sundays I get up early and go to Mass, of course, although the mistress has sometimes tried to get me to attend their Protestant services. Don't worry, I wouldn't set foot in one of their churches -- I'd be afraid for my eternal soul if I did! On Sunday afternoons Mary and I go visiting the other Irish girls we've met, and on Thursday nights we go to dances.

Hundreds of girls and boys from the old country go to the dances. You should see the way the girls dress! You'd think they were all High Society women, the way they drape themselves in all the latest fashions, and I think many of them spend all their pay on fine clothes. Mary is just like them, and I often tell her that she'll end up a poor old woman at this rate. She says she won't have to worry, because she'll find a man to marry and they'll settle down in America. That is not in my plans, as you all know. I count the days till I can come back to you all.

I hear about dear old Ireland more often than you may think, because there are quite a few familiar faces here. Molly McMahon from Creagh is here, as well as her sister Brigid, and the Maher sisters and their cousin Jenny Morrison. They get letters from home quite often, and they keep me up to date on things.

It seems that there is always news of more trouble in our land. Now I hear of more bombings in Britain, carried out by the Fenians, who are agitating for a free Ireland. I worry that the distress and bloodshed will spread to our dear old Skibbereen. Please be safe, I don't know what I would do if anything happened to any of you.

Father, I hear that Mum has been having a lot of her spells lately. Please send Brian out to find her, so that she does not catch cold from roaming about all night. I hope your aches and pains are not too bad.

I pray that Brian and the girls are keeping up with their studies, such as they are. It's a shame the parish school was closed, but they can still practice their reading and writing at home. It's important to have learning in this world. The country over here is a big and confusing place if you don't have some learning to make sense of it all.

I wanted to ask about a person from home. I have been thinking of him a lot, and I wondered if you had heard anything about him. He was the tall black-haired boy who sang "Dear Old Skibbereen" at my American Wake. His name was Sean McCarthy, and he said he might come to America some day. I've thought of him quite a bit this past year, and I wonder if anyone has heard of him since. I never saw the fellow before the night of my party and I don't know much about him. If you hear anything of him, please write and tell me. It's curious I am what ever happened to Sean McCarthy.

Mary Driscoll does not write home as often as she should. Please tell her family not to worry, that all is well with her.

I miss you all terribly, and I think of you often. I hope this finds you all in good health.

Rose

CHAPTER FIVE

August 1884

"What is your name, boy?" The Lieutenant's face, with its luxuriant auburn mustache and brilliant white teeth, was inches away. He smelled of mustache wax and hair oil, with a slight tang of sweat. He had just come in from riding.

"Smith," Sean answered. "John Smith."

"Are you quite sure?" the Lieutenant said. "Don't lie to me. I'll have Sergeant Billings beat it out of you if you lie."

"McCarthy, Your Honor. Sean McCarthy."

Sean was facing the lean, handsome Lieutenant while the beefy Sergeant Billings held his arms behind him in a viselike grip. The Sergeant had dragged him off his wagon and marched him in to the Lieutenant's office, presenting him with the words: "Sir, this is the Irish scum what made all the men sick with his poisoned liquor."

Sean had been making his weekly stop at the army barracks to sell milk and eggs to the cook when the sergeant saw him.

"Is it true what Sergeant Billings has told me, boy?" the Lieutenant said. "Are you the one who sold tainted liquor to my men?"

"No Your Honor," Sean said. "It wouldn't be me who'd do a thing like that."

"Liar!" Sergeant Billings said. "Tell Lieutenant Charlesworth the truth!" he barked, twisting Sean's arm harder, till he winced in pain.

"I sold no bad poteen," Sean gasped. "It was good when I sold it."

The Lieutenant stroked his mustache, then ran a hand through his sandy hair. There was a picture of him on the desk, next to a large glass paperweight with an etching of Queen Victoria. In the picture, the Lieutenant was wearing his scarlet full dress uniform, with a row of medals on his chest. Sean had seen him riding in the countryside, and he was a grand figure on his large black stallion. There was many a day when Sean had wished he could be like the

Lieutenant. He could not help but admire a man who looked so princely when he was astride a horse.

Because the Lieutenant had just come in from riding, he still had on his black riding boots, which made a clicking sound on the wood floor as he paced back and forth. Sean looked down at his own dirty bare feet, and felt ashamed.

"I am aware that my men have been buying what is commonly known as poteen, or home-brewed liquor, from the townspeople around here," the Lieutenant said. "Although I have warned them about the dangers of this practice, it seems they have been doing it anyway."

He was carrying a riding crop, and he held it tightly in one hand and struck it softly against the other. Sean was expecting a blow from that crop at any minute. You have only yourself to blame, boyo, he thought. The old man in the mountains, Murphy, told you it was risky using cow manure to speed up the fermentation process, but you pressed him to do it anyway. Now, you made some of Britain's finest sick, and you'll have hell to pay.

"Admit it, you dirty Irish pig," Sergeant Billings said, his mouth inches from Sean's ear, as he twisted Sean's arm again. "You did it on purpose. It would be just like you Irish scoundrels to try to poison us."

Sean winced again. "It wouldn't be my wish to poison the likes of you, Your Honor. You're here to protect us, aren't you? To keep order among the wild Irish tribes? Why would I try to poison you, then?"

He had to stifle a laugh, though, at the thought of the British soldiers drinking poteen that was fermented with cow manure. Instead, he smiled at the Lieutenant, trying his best to look as innocent as a babe.

The Lieutenant strode up once more to within inches of Sean's face. His cold blue eyes had an intense light in them and there was a vein that was twitching in his neck.

"Have you ever heard of Isandlwana, laddie? It's a place in South Africa where I was stationed a few years ago. We were there to protect British citizens against the Zulu tribes who wanted nothing better than to kill them all. We got ourselves into a bit of a fight at this Isandlwana, and because of some poor leadership at the top we found ourselves in a position of disadvantage. There were little more than a thousand of us, facing twelve thousand Zulu." He paused, and Sean could see his lip twitching now. "Slaughter. We were slaughtered, boy. I was one of only 55 who escaped."

He turned and walked away, then continued talking with his back to Sean. "A British officer is not supposed to survive such engagements. Fight to the last man, and all that. Because the Army doesn't quite know what to do with the survivors of such a bloody embarrassment, they have sent me to this backwater, this hole in the wall."

He turned and strode back, his eyes wild with rage. "So I'm stuck here in a shabby little town like Tullamore in this godforsaken country, a place that spawns people who set off bombs in the heart of London.

"I have had to deal with you thieving, lying, superstitious lot," he continued, "while the fellows I went to school with are off gaining honors and promotions on the battlefield. I have endured more than any military man should have to bear, you see. I am quickly running out of patience with this situation, my dear fellow, and you don't want to cross me. I want you to tell me the name of the man who made that whiskey, and I want it now."

"I don't know his name," Sean said.

Sergeant Billings twisted harder this time, and Sean felt the pain shoot through his arm all the way up to his shoulder. He cried out in agony.

"Tell the Lieutenant!" Billings shouted again in Sean's ear. "Tell him the name now!"

"I don't know it," Sean said, gasping in pain. "I swear I don't." He knew if he told them Murphy's name the next question would be "Where does he live?", and they'd send a detachment of men up in the mountains to get him. He knew also that the old man would never be taken alive. They'd have to kill him, and that would be the end of the only person who'd ever taken an interest in him, who'd virtually adopted him when his father ran off years ago and his mother died.

"You look like an intelligent fellow," the Lieutenant said, trying another tack. "You're young, and I'm sure you have a decent future in front of you. Perhaps you'll even go to America some day, like so many of your countrymen. I wouldn't blame you if you did: I couldn't blame anyone for leaving this vile country. However, you won't have the opportunity to do much of anything if I turn Sergeant Billings loose on you. He's beaten the life out of bigger men than you. Now, tell me the name of the man who made that whiskey."

Billings twisted harder again this time, till Sean almost thought he would faint from the pain. He bit his lip to keep from screaming, and he shook his head no.

This seemed to enrage the Lieutenant more, and he came up in Sean's face again. "What did you say your name was?"

"McCarthy, sir. Sean McCarthy."

"Just another mick," the Sergeant said.

"Yes," the Lieutenant said. "There are so many of them, all with the same bare feet and dirty faces. Well, I suppose you've had your fun, McCarthy. You made quite a number of the Queen's finest very ill from drinking your poisoned liquor. Think of this, however, my fine fellow: You can laugh all you want at your joke, but in point of fact nothing has changed. You are still a filthy Irish nobody, a nothing, a cipher, and your little prank means not a thing. You have succeeded at nothing. You will still lead your miserable existence here for years to come, and the British Army will still be in control in this blasted country. Do you understand?"

"Yes, Your Honor," Sean said.

"Very well," the Lieutenant said. "Sergeant Billings, I will leave you to your devices. I ask only that you take him out back. I do not want blood on the furniture in here."

"Yes, sir," Billings said. "With pleasure, sir."

The Lieutenant strode out of the room, his boots clicking on the floor, and slammed the door when he went out.

Billings shoved Sean toward the back door, but in doing so he released his grip and Sean reached over and picked up the heavy glass paperweight from the desk, then turned and hit Billings square on the side of the head with it.

Billings went down heavily, and before he could get up Sean was on him. He hit the Sergeant again and again with the paperweight, hearing the crack of the man's cheekbone as he hammered the paperweight home.

He didn't know how many times he hit the big Sergeant, but when he finally stopped, panting for breath, he saw the man's face was covered in blood. Billings was unconscious, but he was moaning softly through a broken, bloody face.

Lord, it looks like I've hurt him bad, Sean realized.

Just then the front door opened and the Lieutenant strode in.

"Billings, what is this infernal racket? I thought I told you to take him out back."

There was an instant when the Lieutenant froze, taking in the scene of the large soldier on the floor, the blood, Sean crouching over the big man with a bloody paperweight in his hand.

And then Sean sprang up and launched himself headfirst into the Lieutenant's midsection, knocking him backward into a bookcase, which collapsed, scattering books everywhere. He still had the paperweight in his hand and he crawled on top of the Lieutenant and began to pound him in the face with it just like he'd done to Billings. He was like a man possessed, and he lost track of time while he kept hitting the other man again and again, till eventually he realized the Lieutenant had stopped struggling and was lying still.

Somehow, Sean came to his senses. He looked down at the silent, bloody man on the floor.

What have I done?

Oh, God, he's dead. He must be dead, for he's lying so still.

Sean looked at the blood-spattered paperweight in his hand and suddenly threw it across the room, where it clattered off the wall.

Slowly his mind began to function again, and he assessed the situation coldly, as if he was watching someone else's life.

Sean McCarthy, you've killed an officer of the British Crown. You will be sentenced to death, and you will hang for this.

There is no alternative.

You must get away.

Sergeant Billings was still moaning on the floor, but he was starting to move about, and it looked like he would be on his feet soon.

Sean jumped up, intending to make a mad dash out of the building.

No, wait. If I run out of here like that I'll attract attention. The soldiers will be on me in an instant. I must act calm, like nothing unusual has happened.

He looked at his bloody hands. That won't do. He wiped the blood off on the Lieutenant's uniform. He straightened his clothes, took a deep breath, and walked out the front door, opening it carefully to scan the area in front.

The Lieutenant's office and quarters were down a dirt road from the long, low building where the soldiers were quartered. There was nobody outside, and all was quiet. Most of the soldiers were probably in their bunks, recovering from the bad whiskey.

Sean walked slowly outside, then tried to be casual as he sauntered over to his little cart with his ancient brown horse tied to it. He picked up the reins, got up on the cart, and rode slowly out of the barracks area and down the path leading toward the countryside. He would not go into the town of Tullamore; there were British shopkeepers there, and someone might get suspicious if they saw blood on him.

No, he would go back to the mountain, to Murphy. Murphy would tell him what to do. He would fix it somehow. He was an old, half-blind, ague-ridden man, but he had wisdom. Sean had to get back to Murphy, for somehow the old man would know what to do.

But Murphy looked at him with sad eyes in the flickering light of the peat fire in his cabin and said, "You must leave, Sean McCarthy."

"Leave Tullamore? I suppose I could go down south, to Cork. There's a girl I knew there once, it's a fine country, and the people are of good stock. Or I could go out west, where the country is wild. They'd never find me there."

"They'd find you anywhere on this green island," Murphy said. "You've killed one of their own, boyo. They won't rest till they catch you. No, you must leave this country, forever."

"Where will I go?" Sean said. "Canada? Australia?"

"No," the old man said. "The hand of Britain is too strong in those countries. You must go to America. It's a roaring big country, with none of the Queen's business about it, and they won't find you there."

"America," Sean repeated. "Sure and I couldn't do that. Most people who go there never come back. It would mean leaving my home forever."

"And why not?" said Murphy. "You have no family here, save me, and I'm an old man who won't be around much longer. Look at you, lad. You haven't a decent pair of shoes, nor clothes except those rags on your back. You have nothing here. America's a land where you can start afresh. Why, people tell me you can be whatever you want there, there's opportunity for all. Maybe you'll get a chance to use that fine voice you have. You can be a singer, or a businessman, or some other fine thing, and live in a grand house with servants of your own."

"Where will I get the money for the passage?" Sean said.

Murphy went to a dark corner of the cabin and lifted a plank, then rooted around in a hole in the floor. He pulled out a red kerchief, brought it over and threw it in Sean's lap. "Here you are, my boyo," he said. "It's the money I've made from selling the poteen these last years. There should be enough in there for your ticket, and then some more to get you on your way once you get there."

"Thank you," Sean said, overcome at the old man's generosity. "It's grateful I am to you."

"Don't mention it," Murphy said. "Use another name while you're traveling, though. Just to be sure the authorities don't catch on to you."

"Where will I go?" Sean said. "America is a big place."

"I hear Philadelphia is a good city," Murphy said. "Lots of our kind there."

"Philadelphia," Sean said. "Yes, that's the place. It might be that I'll know someone there."

CHAPTER SIX

June 1886

"You can scoff all you like, dear Rose," Mary said, "but I know what I see: young Mr. Lancaster has taken a liking to you." Mary and Rose were taking Victoria and Tom, the two younger Lancaster children, on a shopping trip prior to Victoria's European excursion with her mother. The trip to Europe was an 18th birthday present and Mrs. Lancaster was taking her daughter on a grand tour of cities like Paris, London, and Milan. She had sent Victoria to buy a few more dresses before their ship sailed in two days.

They were at Wanamaker's Grand Depot on Market Street in Philadelphia, and Victoria was trying on dresses while Tom was busy in the toy department.

"Don't talk such nonsense," Rose said, feeling the color rising to her face. "Martin Lancaster would never be interested in me. Why, his mother would be appalled and his father would disown him."

"You know I'm telling the truth," Mary said, fingering some Parisian lace that was on display. "I see the way he looks at you. Have you not noticed it yourself? He gets all pink in the face, like a silly young girl. And he's always looking for excuses to do things with you. Do you not remember the snowball fight in April? It was comical, the way he got so upset when young Tom hit you in the face with one of them snowballs."

Rose did remember that incident, very well. Snow was a rarity in Ireland, and when there was a Spring blizzard in Philadelphia a few months back, Rose and Mary could not resist scampering about in the foot-high drifts around the house with Tom and Victoria. They pushed each other down in the snow, laughing madly, and then started to pelt each other with snowballs. Martin came outside just as Tom had hit Rose in the face with a hard-packed snowball and knocked her down.

Martin swore at his little brother and ran over to Rose, lifting her gently to her feet and putting his arm around her. Rose was not hurt badly, and she was shocked by the tenderness Martin showed her.

"Are you all right, dear Rose?" he had said. "I'm sorry if that scamp of a brother of mine hurt you."

"I'm fine, Mr. Lancaster," Rose said, trying to make light of it. "No damage done."

"You've received a bad bruise to your cheek," he said. "We should bandage it up." He took Rose inside to the kitchen and made her sit down while he put tincture of iodine on the wound and then a bandage of heavy gauze with tape over it. The way he worked on her with such concern and tenderness was embarrassing, and she kept trying to get him to stop.

"Why, he was just trying to help me," Rose said to Mary. "He thought I was hurt badly."

"You can think that if you want," Mary said, merrily. "But I know when a man looks at a woman that way it means a good deal more."

"And I suppose you've had men look at you that way!" Rose said.

"More than one," Mary said, winking at her. "After all, I don't live like a nun, like you do. I've had men take a fancy to me, and I know what it feels like. You would too if you ever went out and had a bit of a social life."

Rose tried to change the subject. "Look at old Mansfield out there, with the carriage," she said, pointing through the window to an old man in a coachman's black coat who was standing next to a carriage on the street. "He's taking another nip."

As they watched the tall, thin old man glanced about him to see if anyone was looking, then pulled a flask out of his pocket, opened it, and took a long swallow of the contents. He shivered once with pleasure, then corked the flask and put it back in his pocket.

"The old sot," Mary said. "He's been hitting that bottle more than usual. It makes me nervous about driving with him. I'm half expecting him to topple the carriage one of these days."

"I don't know why Mrs. Lancaster puts up with him," Rose said. "He's not in a fit state to drive the carriage most days."

"I think he was put on notice after the last accident," Mary said. "One more time and they'll cut him loose."

"Mary, can you come here?" Victoria called, from the other end of the Ladies' Dresses department. "I need your advice about something."

Mary smiled broadly, and Rose whispered, "Well, I guess you're pleased, when the young mistress asks your advice about fine clothes."

"At least she knows which one of us to ask," Mary said, winking. "It wouldn't do any good to ask your advice, since you dress like a washerwoman." She sashayed off to give Victoria her advice, with a playful toss of her head.

"What is this world coming to," Rose muttered, "when a fine young woman like Mistress Lancaster is asking the likes of Mary Driscoll for advice about fashion?"

When Victoria had made her decision and it was time to go, Rose found young Tom in the toy department and they all made their way outside to the carriage.

Old Mansfield seemed rather groggy by now, with a red nose and watery eyes. When he helped Rose into the carriage after the others she smelled liquor on his breath. Tom held his nose in the carriage, and Victoria raised her eyes to heaven, realizing their coachman was drunk again.

Mansfield took the reins and the horses moved out, heading off in the direction of the new City Hall building, where they would turn and go up Broad Street toward their destination at the edge of the city. The streets were crowded with carriages and people hurrying everywhere, great commercial wagons rumbling by, streetcars clanking along the tracks, policemen with their whistles directing traffic, all the myriad sights and sounds of the great city. It was so different than the quiet life Rose had known in Skibbereen, and even though she had been in America for six years now, she was still thrilled and appalled by it.

The carriage passed by the great white wedding cake of the City Hall building, with its high tower and many windows reflecting the brilliant June sunshine, and Mansfield made the turn onto Broad Street. Off to the side of the street there was a work crew, the men down a hole below the street level, digging with their shirts off.

All of a sudden there was a loud explosion near the work crew. The force of it rocked the carriage, and the horses screamed and reared up. Rose saw a ball of fire rising up from the hole, and heard a fierce hissing sound, and then the horses took off. There was a cacophony of sounds: screaming women, horses whinnying in terror, the sound of carriages colliding as horses panicked, and more explosions. Rose, Mary, Victoria and Tom were thrown together inside the carriage as the horses took it on a wild ride. Mansfield was trying to regain control of them, but he seemed disoriented and could only manage a feeble, "Ho, there!" as he pulled on the reins.

"What's going on?" Victoria shouted. "Stop the carriage, Mansfield!"

But the carriage was out of control. It was careening down a cobblestoned side street, the horses galloping madly. There was a dead end at the bottom of the street, with a large brick building in the way, and the horses wheeled and turned, tilting the carriage crazily on two wheels. They galloped back toward Broad Street, then turned and headed for the dead end again. Each time they turned the carriage felt like it was going to fall over, till Rose thought they surely were about to crash and be spilled out on the sidewalk like so many sacks of flour.

Rose stuck her head out the window to see what Mansfield was doing, and got the shock of her life. The old man was slumped in his seat, his head down and the reins slack in his hand. The horses were galloping out of control, and there was no one to calm them down.

We're done for, she thought. With a team of out of control horses and a driver who was unconscious, it was a certainty they'd crash now, and possibly die.

Then something happened. All of a sudden someone jumped on the seat next to Mansfield and grabbed the reins. Rose could see it was a bare-chested man, and she guessed it was one of the ditch diggers. He shouted to the horses and pulled firmly on the reins, and immediately the carriage slowed down. Somehow he threaded their way through the crowded street and then turned the carriage onto a small, narrow alley and coaxed the horses to a stop. He jumped down, and went around to the front of them and tied their leads to a post, then put his face close to theirs and whispered to them in a soothing voice to get them to calm down. In a moment, they stopped snorting and tossing their heads, and simply stood there, panting heavily, but calm.

Victoria was crying uncontrollably, and Tom was agog, wanting to get out and see what was happening on the main thoroughfare. There were cries for help now, and a fire wagon was ringing its bell frantically. From the sound of it, there were people in desperate straits at the scene of the accident.

"Let me out!" Tom cried. "I want to see what's going on."

"You won't do any such thing, young man," Mary said. "It's dangerous out there, and you'll not be larking about while there's explosions going on."

Rose held Victoria close and tried to calm her, and eventually the girl's sobs diminished.

"Who was that man who saved us?" she said. "I want to thank him. We could have been killed." Before she could get out of the carriage, however, the man appeared at their door.

"Are you all right?" he asked. "Is anyone hurt?"

He was a tall, black-haired man with piercing blue eyes, and he had a red bandana tied around his head. He was covered in dirt and sweat, but Rose knew him instantly.

It was Sean McCarthy.

CHAPTER SEVEN

A light flashed in Sean McCarthy's eyes when he saw Rose, and she felt a bolt of lightning go through her body. She knew that he recognized her. He gave her a sly wink, however, which seemed to caution her not to let on that she knew him.

"It looks like we survived," Rose said. "There are no injuries here."

"We are in your debt, sir," Victoria said. "You have saved us from certain death."

"It's nothing," Sean said. "Those poor horses got the bejesus scared out of them, and it was just a matter of calming them down. I'm afraid your driver fainted dead away, though, ma'am. He has a bad cut on his head and he's bleeding like a pig. I think he's coming around now, but he'll need medical attention."

"Mansfield, hurt?" Victoria said. "The poor old man."

"He was drunk!" Tom shouted. "He could have killed us."

"Hush, don't be disrespectful," Mary said. "It's just glad I am that we didn't all die."

She did not seem to recognize Sean, and Rose was glad, because Sean did not seem to want to be recognized.

"What on earth happened back there?" Mary said, looking to Sean for an explanation.

"Yes, tell us!" Tom said. "Something blew up. What happened?"

"I think one of the lads in my crew hit a gas line with his pick," Sean said. "I heard a whistling sound, and then there was an explosion. One of the bosses was smoking a cigar, and I think a spark from it caught fire. Lucky it was for me, I was taking a break and wasn't in the hole with them when it happened.

"What will we do?" Victoria wailed. "Mother will be worried sick if she hears about this."

"I'll drive you home," Sean offered. "I can handle horses pretty well, and I'll make sure you get home safely. I'd better take care of your coachman, first, though. There will be police and medical people out there on Broad Street. I'll take the old boy over and see if they can help him."

Rose marveled at the way he had changed. Sean McCarthy was no longer a boy; he was a full-grown man with a robust body and a commanding presence. He helped Mansfield off the carriage, and half-carried the old man back out to Broad Street to get him some medical attention. Mansfield was blinking his eyes and gaping as if he were waking up from a dream, and his face was covered in blood.

"So sorry," Mansfield mumbled, as Sean led him away. "So terribly sorry."

"The poor man," Victoria said.

"I wouldn't worry too much about him," Mary said. "He probably isn't feeling any pain right now."

Sean was gone awhile, and since Tom had such a powerful urge to see what happened, Mary took him and Victoria down the alley to survey the scene of the accident. Rose told them she'd stay with the carriage, and when they were gone she tried to calm her pounding heart.

Sean McCarthy. Here. It was hard to believe it was really true. It had been six years since Rose left Ireland, six years since she'd last seen him. In all those years she had never stopped thinking of him. She'd written home many times asking if anyone had seen or heard of him, but no one had. Often at night she would lie in bed and imagine his kiss on her lips, his clear singing voice, his inky black hair and those piercing blue eyes. She felt the hunger in her heart again for him, the way she'd felt it back in Skibbereen.

She had met other Irish men at the dances, and many had been interested in her. She had matured into a "handsome young woman" as Mary called her. She had long auburn hair and a creamy complexion, and green eyes with long red lashes. None of the men appealed to her, though. "You'll grow old waiting for that McCarthy boy," Mary would say, urging her to show an interest in someone else. "Sure, and he's probably met a fair colleen back in Ireland, and he's married now and slaving away on his little plot of land, growing his potatoes and falling behind in his rent to the landlord."

Rose remembered how he'd said, "Don't be surprised if you see me there before long." She knew it was foolish to think this way about someone she'd only met once, for a fleeting hour the night before she left for America, but her heart would not let her forget him.

There was something dangerous about him, though. He was a man who could upset the most carefully laid plans. She had been sending money home regularly, and she had a plan that in four more years she would be boarding a ship to go home to her family. Now that Sean McCarthy was here, she could feel her grip on that plan loosening.

When he came back to the carriage, he had put on a blue work shirt and an old straw hat set at a jaunty angle, and he'd cleaned his face off. He was laughing about something he'd just said to young Tom, and it gave Rose a thrill to see the way his broad smile lit up his face.

She tried to hide it by putting on a stern face. "What are the two of you laughing about?" she said. "We almost got killed, and there could be people out there on Broad Street who were unluckier than us. It's not a time for laughter."

"Begging your pardon, ma'am," Sean said. "But things turned out better than expected, by the grace of God. No one has been killed. There are some people hurt, but they've already been taken to hospital. That's where your man Mansfield is, by the way. And I was just telling young Master Thomas here that this gives me an excuse to get off from digging in a dank hole all afternoon and instead take a drive to the country."

"I hope you can drive as well as you say you can," Mary said, as they got into the carriage. "We've had quite enough reckless driving for one afternoon."

"Oh, don't worry about me, ma'am," Sean said. "I had a lot of practice driving horses in my home country. I'm a master at it."

"He certainly doesn't lack for confidence," Mary said, as Sean leaped into the driver's seat, made a space for Tom to sit next to him, then took the reins and called to the horses to start them off.

Rose was amazed that Mary still hadn't recognized Sean, but she sat back and tried to keep her emotions veiled for the ride home. Sean was, true to what he said, a very capable driver of horses, and with Tom sitting next to him and telling him where to turn, they made it home to Chestnut Hill without a problem.

When they got there Mr. Lancaster was frantically pacing the front porch, with his wife sitting next to him and crying into her handkerchief. Both of them came running when they saw the carriage headed up the long driveway.

"Father, Mother, we were in an explosion!" Tom shouted, before they had reached the carriage, and he jumped down and ran to his mother, who was almost hysterical with fright.

She held him tightly and screamed, "Is Victoria all right? Where is Victoria? And Mary and Rose?"

"We're fine, missus," Mary said, getting out when Sean pulled the carriage to a stop. "Nobody's hurt, thank the Lord."

"Someone came to the office and told us about a gas main explosion," Mr. Lancaster said. "I knew you were going shopping in town today, and I rushed over to Wanamaker's, but the scene was pure chaos, with injured people everywhere and horses panicking. I could not find you, so I took the first train home, hoping you would turn up here."

"Father, it was so frightening," Victoria said, getting out of the carriage. "The horses stampeded and we thought we would surely die, but this noble man here saved us. He took control of the carriage when Mansfield had a fainting spell--"

"He was drunk!" Tom said.

"I don't know what caused his spell," Victoria said, "but the fact is he was unconscious and the horses were out of control. This man saved us."

"What is your name, young man?" Mr. Lancaster said. "I am eternally grateful to you."

Sean had gotten down from the carriage and was holding the reins. He gave a quick glance at Rose, and then said: "My name is Peter Morley, your honor. I'm a son of Erin, from County Tyrone. I'm still new to this fine country, but I couldn't sit by and watch those horses go wild like that. The terrible noise of the explosion put them in a fright. They could have hurt themselves or someone else. All they needed was someone to take control of them."

"He's a good driver," Tom said. "Why don't you hire him? He'd be a better driver than Mansfield. At least he wouldn't be drunk every time we go out."

"Hush, Tom," Mary said. "The old man likes to tipple, 'tis true, but you shouldn't be talking about him like that. After all, he's in the hospital at this very moment, and deserves our prayers."

"Is he hurt gravely?" Mrs. Lancaster said.

"No, ma'am," Sean said. "He has some cuts and bruises, but I believe the old boy will survive."

"I have known about Mansfield's habits for quite a while," Mr. Lancaster said, his face reddening. "I should have dealt with this before now, but I tried to show him Christian charity. Alas, this is the fruit of my efforts: the man almost got my dear daughter and son killed. I will pay for his medical bills, and I will give him a generous payment for his services, but from this day forward he is gone from my employ."

"You'll be needing a coachman, then," Sean spoke up. "I'd like to apply for the job, Your Honor. I'm a good man with horses, and I don't drink on the job. And you may not be able to tell just now, but when I get cleaned up I cut a fine figure in a coachman's uniform." He smiled and winked, and Mr. Lancaster laughed.

"Why not, Father?" Tom said. "I think he'd be a good coachman."

Mr. Lancaster studied Sean for a moment. "You're a man of good character?" he said.

"The best, Your Honor," Sean said.

"You haven't asked me what the pay is," Mr. Lancaster said.

"I leave that up to you, sir," Sean said, bowing grandly. "Whatever you think is fitting."

Mr. Lancaster looked at his wife. "What do you think, my dear? Does he seem like he'd be a good coachman?"

Mrs. Lancaster looked at Sean. It was obvious she was still struggling with the residue of the fear, worry, and finally joy that was brought on by the afternoon's events, and amid all these emotions playing on her features, at last she smiled and said: "This man saved our children. I think we can take that as proof of his good character."

"Then, you are hired," Mr. Lancaster said. "I will pay you a wage of six dollars a week, the same I paid to Mansfield. You can have his room also. Can you start immediately?"

"Yes, to be sure," Sean said. "I can start as soon as I collect my few belongings from the rooming house I stay at downtown. I can assure you, sir, that you won't regret this decision. You'll find no better coachman than myself."

"Hurrah!" said Tom. "We are all happy to have Peter join the family."

"Perhaps this explosion will turn out to be a good thing," Mr. Lancaster said. "In that it has brought Peter to us."

Rose felt her heart jump, and she had to quickly turn away to control her emotions. To have Sean McCarthy living in the same house as her after so many years apart from him was almost too much to take in.

And yet, a part of her wondered if it really was a good thing.

CHAPTER EIGHT

He was Peter now, not Sean. He had chosen the name on the dock at Cork, where he bought the ticket on the ship that brought him to America. When the ticket agent asked him his name, he knew not to say, "Sean McCarthy", for the soldiers would be looking for that person. He chose "Peter" because it was the old moonshiner Murphy's first name, and he wanted to honor the man who'd been like a father to him. The last name, "Morley", he'd gotten from a store across the street from the dock: Morley's Apothecary.

It was amazing how quickly he'd gotten used to the new name. He introduced himself as Peter Morley to people on board the ship, and he made up a story about himself, that he was from County Tyrone in the north and he was going to America to find his cousin, who was working in the building trade in America. He kept the conversation going so that nobody had time to ask too many questions about his past, but that was an easy matter for he enjoyed talking with people and entertaining them with his stories.

When the ship docked in Philadelphia he strode off it feeling as if he were a new man. His old life was gone, and he meant to embrace this new one with gusto. He marveled at the sights and sounds all around him: the crowds of people hurrying everywhere; the mechanical wonders like the street cars and electric lights; the stores crammed with products and gadgets of all descriptions; the markets spilling over with things like blueberries, corn and apples that were new to his eyes; and the cacophony of languages he heard from conversations all around him.

It was a wonderland, and he walked around for weeks in an ecstasy, like the saints of old, amazed at everything he saw and heard and smelled and tasted. It seemed like a man could be anything here, and he saw the opportunity to become a grand, fine man, someone who was respected and admired, someone rather than no one, which is what he'd always been.

He had to start out small, of course. It was only natural that he'd scrape along looking for work and finding only the lowest jobs available, jobs that Americans didn't want. He got a job cleaning outhouses, then another one cleaning out stables. It was a step up when he finally got a job digging ditches. He never complained, kept his spirits up, waiting for his chance to present itself.

When the gas main broke and the explosion occurred, he was strangely calm. He saw the runaway carriage and jumped aboard it almost without thinking. He had always been good with horses, and he quickly got the team under control, and guided them down an alley.

When he got off the carriage and saw Rose Sullivan he was thunderstruck. To see her again, the girl from Skibbereen, to recognize that girl and yet to see how she'd grown into a beautiful young woman, was captivating. But then there was another realization: that Rose was working for a wealthy family in Philadelphia, and maybe this would be the opportunity he was looking for.

It had worked out just the way he wanted. He was hired to be the family's coachman, and he got to live in the big house with them, in a room off the kitchen. He got to wear a fine uniform with a long black coat, and he felt proud of the way he looked in it. He ate meals in the kitchen with the help, and they were better than the slop he'd been eating in the rooming house. He made the princely sum of six dollars a week.

And he was near Rose. It was an amazement to him that in all of this great big country he'd ended up in the same house with the girl from Skibbereen he'd kissed that summer evening years ago. She was more beautiful now than she'd been that night, and his heart quickened when he was near her. From the way she acted around him, her face all red and pink, her breath coming in short bursts, and how she seemed too nervous to speak, he knew she had feelings for him too.

He had a rival, though. The Lancaster's eldest son, Martin, who was on summer vacation from his law studies at the University of Pennsylvania, was clearly interested in Rose. It was shocking to Peter, because in Ireland the fine people rarely stooped to show that kind of interest in a simple housemaid like Rose.

But he was definitely sweet on her. He was a fair-haired man with Anglo-Saxon features and a fine thin nose, and he had that grace and charm that seemed to be bred into the upper classes. He treated Rose like a delicate flower, always showing interest in her workaday duties, embarrassing her with his attentions. At times

Peter had walked in on them in the kitchen or some other part of the house, and they would be in the middle of a hushed conversation, which always ended in Rose getting pink in the face when she saw Peter, and then rushing out.

It was difficult for Peter to get a moment with her alone. She worked from dawn till late at night, and his duties with the horses and carriages kept him busy. It took weeks before he was able to get five minutes with her to explain why he'd changed his name to Peter Morley. He didn't tell her the whole truth, of course. He simply said he'd gotten into some trouble with the authorities at home, and he thought it better to change his identity.

He tried not to think of what happened back there in Tullamore. It was a painful memory, like so many of his memories from the old country, and he pushed it away. He knew he should go to Confession and tell a priest that he'd killed two men. The priest would tell him to turn himself in to the authorities, to receive his earthly punishment for his sins.

He could not do that.

He knew the punishment would be a hanging, and he could not condemn himself to a fate like that.

Better that Sean McCarthy should die, and Peter Morley be born. He was starting fresh here; the past was dead. Once, as a boy he'd seen the crest of Tullamore in the town hall. It showed a phoenix rising from the ashes, which referred to the town's rebirth after a terrible fire that had destroyed it a hundred years before. He took that crest as his own; he would be that phoenix, he decided, and rise from the ashes of his former life.

He would be reborn.

A month after he started work for the Lancasters he went on a Sunday afternoon excursion with Rose. Mrs. Lancaster had gone off to Europe with Victoria, and Tom had been sent on the train to visit his grandparents in New York. Mr. Lancaster and Martin were out attending a base ball game in the city.

Sunday afternoons the staff had off, and Mary came to Peter on Saturday and said, "Rose and I made plans for a picnic tomorrow. Would you like to come? My friend James O'Toole is coming, and we thought you might like to join us."

He was only too happy to join them. He took a hot bath to get the smell of the stable off him, shaved, brushed his hair carefully, and wore a brown wool suit that he'd bought with his first week's pay. He joined Rose and Mary and they met James O'Toole, a bluff, hearty fellow who worked for a family in Germantown, at the train station.

They were taking a train into town, then they were going to take a walk in the grounds of the Laurel Hill cemetery and picnic on one of its bluffs overlooking the Schuylkill River. Mary was dressed in all her finery, with a bonnet trimmed in red and blue, and a creamy pale yellow French silk blouse, with a blue serge skirt that had ruffles on the bottom, and she was carrying a pale blue silk parasol to protect her from the July sun. Rose was dressed more plainly in a prim blue bonnet, but she wore a green pendant around her neck that matched her green eyes and was reflected by the pale green shirtwaist she wore that was buttoned all the way up to her graceful neck. She wore a black skirt that came down to the tops of her high-buttoned shoes.

Peter was entranced. He had never seen women dressed like this, and to be strolling about in the open air with two women like this was magical. It was a beautiful afternoon, and they joined hundreds of people out for a stroll in the cemetery, among the stone monuments, statues, and mausoleums belonging to the great and famous people who were buried there.

They picnicked near the monument to Matthias Baldwin, the founder of the great Baldwin Locomotive Works, a company that built thousands of the steam powered locomotives that had brought progress to every corner of this country.

"Imagine," Peter said, looking at the great stone obelisk atop Baldwin's monument. "This man's company built the steam engine that brought us here. That's a man who's done something in his life."

"Aye," James said, "but he's buried here like all the rest. He might have built a fine big company, and made a pile of money, but he's ended up where we all will in time." He was sitting on a blanket eating his lunch, and he waved a chicken leg to make his point.

"True," Peter said, "but that company he started is carrying on his name. It's right there on every steam engine: 'Baldwin Locomotive Works'. So, he lives on, you see."

"And what good does it do him?" James said. "He's dead and gone."

"Well, he died knowing his name would live on," Peter said. "It's a sight better than most of us have to console us on our dying day."

"Peter Morley, you're talking like a pagan," Mary said, between bites of her own chicken leg. You know we Catholics believe we'll all be reunited in Heaven, by God's grace. What value is a name on a locomotive against the hope of eternal life?"

Peter looked off at the blue river below and said, "Ah, we can't all be sure of that, Mary. Even if the priests are right, it's not all of us will go to Heaven. Some will be condemned to Hell for their sins."

"And what sins do you have, that you're talking of Hell?" Mary said. "It's not in my future, I'll tell you that. I'm not a saint, God knows, but I've done nothing to condemn me to the fires of Hell. Unless admiring a handsome man is a sin these days." She winked at James, who smiled and winked back.

"And what of you, Rose?" Mary said. "Don't you have anything to say about this?"

Rose had been reclining on the warm green grass with her eyes closed, but apparently she was paying attention to the conversation. "You sound like Father Flaherty in church, with all this talk of Heaven and Hell."

"Well, what is it, Rose Sullivan?" Peter said. "I'd like to know where you stand on this. Don't you wish to have people remember your name when you're gone?"

Rose sat up and stared at him. "To my mind, that's the benefit of family. It's something bigger than us all, family is. That's why I'm going back to my family in a few more years. Sullivans have lived around Skibbereen for ages past -- why, the graveyard is full of Sullivans -- and they'll be there ages from now. It makes me happy to think I'm part of that."

"Not me," Mary said. "I'll not go back there and live on potatoes and turnips again. I have finer tastes than that."

"Marry me, fine Mary," said James, winking at her, "and I'll keep you in champagne and steak the rest of your days."

"The nonsense you talk, Mr. O'Toole!" Mary said, giggling.

"Shall we take a walk down by the river, Mary?" James said. "It's a fine afternoon, and I'd like to enjoy it down by the water."

"Aye," Mary said, "If you promise not to get my fine clothes all wet."

"I'm the soul of good behavior," James said, lifting his eyes to Heaven. "You can trust me, my girl."

"That'll be the death of me, trusting handsome fellows like you," Mary said, "but let's go anyway."

They left and there was an awkward silence while Rose looked after them.

Peter sat down next to her and said, "Rose, I admire you for your loyalty, but I'm of the same opinion as Mary. I would not go back to our fair isle now if the Queen herself invited me back. This country holds too much promise. Why, a man can be anything he wants to be here."

"I don't want to be anything but myself," Rose said. "I know who I am, and that's Rose Sullivan from Skibbereen.

"And who are you?" she said, looking him right in the eye. "Are you Sean McCarthy or Peter Morley? I don't even know your real name."

"It's Peter Morley, now," Peter said. "I told you, there's no more Sean McCarthy. I am Peter here. A new name for a new life," he said, smiling, "but still smitten by the same girl."

Then he leaned over and kissed Rose.

CHAPTER NINE

May 1887

Dear Theresa,

I hope this letter finds everyone in the family in good health and spirits. I am sending another hundred dollars, and I hope you may put it to good use. When you wrote me and said Brian had lost most of the money I sent last year betting on horse races, it made me very sad. I deny myself many pleasures so that I can send that money over to you. I had hoped Father would use it to pay the rent, and perhaps to buy more pigs to raise. I also hoped he would be able to pay for more education for you and Annie. It would be good to get someone to tutor both of you in reading and arithmetic. I don't see how anyone can get along in this world anymore without education. I am glad for the little I got as a girl, but I hope the rest of you can get more.

I am still working for the Lancaster family, and I am happy to be here. They are kind, good people, and I feel welcome in this house. Things have changed in some ways, however.

The biggest change is that Mary Driscoll is no longer working here. It saddens me to say that Mary was dismissed from service last month for stealing. My dear sister, it was a shock to me when I found out that Mary was taking pieces of Mrs. Lancaster's jewelry and selling them to a man of low character who then sold them to others. I found one of Mrs. Lancaster's rings in the room I shared with Mary, and when I asked her about it she told me what she was doing.

Mary blamed it on her latest beau, saying that he had pressured her to steal from her employer. That may be true, but it's also true that Mary has rich tastes. I often wondered how she was able to afford so many beautiful clothes and fine jewelry when she was making a housemaid's wages. Perhaps Mrs. Lancaster also wondered the same thing, because she searched our room one day when we were out, and she found some of her jewelry hidden in Mary's steamer trunk.

When we came back the lady confronted us, and Mary tried to blame it on me. She said I pressured her to steal so that I could make more money to send home to my family. I was shocked to hear those words coming out of Mary's mouth, and I told Mrs. Lancaster it was a lie. Somehow she believed me, and she dismissed Mary on the spot.

Mary took me aside before she left and said I should have taken the blame. "It wouldn't have been so bad for you to be sent home," she said. "You're pining to go back anyway. I can't go back there, Rose Sullivan. I won't be sent back to that sleepy, backward little country and live on scraps the rest of my life, and dress in rags the way they do. Look what you've done, for now God only knows what will happen to me, if I can't work in service."

Poor Mary. Sorry I was for what happened to her, but I could not afford to take the blame for her stealing. Even so, I am afraid I was a bit harsh with her. Perhaps I lectured her over much, for she told me I was acting "holier than Jesus Himself".

It may be true, but I cannot be sent home in disgrace like that, when I've vowed to send money back to all of you.

I have not seen Mary in a month, but I have heard from friends that she has found a man to support her. I have no idea what the circumstances are of this arrangement, and perhaps it's better that I do not know.

The Lancasters have hired another girl to take Mary's place, and she seems pleasant enough, although very green. She has only been in America two months, and she knows nothing. Looking at her, I realize how much I have grown since I've been here. Once I was young and untutored like her, and now I am older and wiser. But perhaps also more weary.

It is a mixed blessing to be here. I am glad to work for such good people, and I am amazed at all the wonders I see in this busy, crowded country, but I miss you all so much even now, after seven years here. I often dream of the green fields and hills of Cork, and the way the great cloud banks roll in from the sea, and how the sun bursts through the clouds after a rainstorm, the shattered pieces of sunlight that reflect off the river and light up the whitewashed houses on the hillsides.

I get along well, though, and I have met a fine Irish man named Peter Morley. He is the coachman for the Lancasters, and he is a handsome, tall fellow with a beautiful singing voice. It is quite a miracle, actually, that he turned up here. He is the boy who sang at my party the night before I left for America. Do you remember him? He was just a boy then, but he has filled out into a sturdy man now.

He called himself Sean McCarthy back then, but now he is known as Peter Morley. He says he got into some trouble in his hometown and that it was better to change his name and leave. He won't tell me what happened, but I suspect it was some type of political activity. I know there is so much turmoil in our land, what with the Land Reform movement and all the people agitating for independence from England, and maybe Peter got caught up in that. It may seem strange to you that a man would change his family name, but I assure you it is not uncommon here. Many of our people do the same thing, either to make it easy for Americans to pronounce their names, or because of misunderstandings. For some it's just a way of starting fresh.

This Peter is a spirited fellow who sees humor in everything, and he makes me laugh and smile whenever he is around. We go to dances, and we take carriage rides, and we go on picnics and excursions on Sunday afternoons. In the summer we take the train to the seashore for the day, to feel the ocean breezes. He brings happiness to my life, and takes away some of the sadness I feel at being separated from you all.

I blush to write this, but he is also quite good at showing his affection through a kiss. He has a way of kissing that almost makes me swoon, and I can hardly get my breath for minutes afterward.

I think that I am in love with him. There, I wrote it! I don't know why it is so difficult to write that word. I never heard Mum and Da say it, so maybe that's the reason. I just know that I think about Peter all the time, and my heart gallops like a runaway horse when he is near. He is such a fine, tall man with a beautiful smile, and he makes me feel happy. He has big plans, and I like to listen to his dreams as he talks about them. He thinks this country is a roaring good place to be, and I get caught up in his enthusiasm when I listen to him. He loves the sense of freedom here, how every man has a reason to think that he can make something of himself. He talks to everyone he meets, and asks about their background. He tells me that many a rich man in this country started out as a poor immigrant, and he aims to do the same thing.

My life is not without complications, however. There is one troubling thing about my situation, and it is that the Lancasters' eldest son Martin has taken an interest in me. He is a fine young man who is studying to be a lawyer, but I do not understand why he feels this way about me. He follows me around and gives me tender looks, and he is always declaring his affection for me. Peter has noticed, and he thinks it amusing, but I am embarrassed by it.

I have tried to dampen Martin Lancaster's ardor by being cool to him, but I am afraid of being too firm, since he is my employer's son. If I give him any reason for encouragement I fear his mother may find out and dismiss me from service. I do not want to lose my position with this family like I did with the Overtons in Pittsburgh. I fear that if I am dismissed again no one will ever want to hire me, and I will have to come back to Ireland in disgrace.

I know that Father would never forgive me if that happened. You may trust that I will not ever bring shame to the family. I go to Mass every Sunday and I say my prayers every night. Our dear Mary fell away from her Faith, and would not go to Mass anymore. I tried to get her to stay faithful, but she did not listen to me. I fear her head is too full of the bustle and excitement of life here, and she forgot the important things, which got her into trouble. She was more interested in the latest fashions and stepping out with her men friends than going to "a stuffy old church" as she called it. Please do not tell her family of this, nor of her stealing, for I do not want them to hear bad things about her. I will continue to pray for her, you may be sure of that.

Theresa, please tell Mum and Da that I love them very much. Please tell Father that I pray for Mother every night. It saddens me to hear that she has been talking so much about fairies and changelings of late.

I often feel guilty about her, because she started her talk about changelings when I was 12 years old, and it was the same age she was during the worst of the Famine. I think somehow I reminded her of herself as a girl, and it brought back terrible memories. She saw evil things during those years, looked Death in the eye many times, and it broke her mind like a glass clock that has been shattered into a thousand pieces.

I hope she is not forgetting to eat again, and that she wears a proper shawl when she goes out, so she doesn't catch cold. Please look after her.

How is Father? I pray his rheumatism is not getting worse. When you told me in your last letter that he walks bent over and with a limp, I could have cried.

Tell Annie to mind what you tell her, and to do her chores with a smiling face. With all the pain that Father has, the least she can do is walk about with a smile on her face each day -- it costs nothing, and it gladdens his heart so.

Tell Brian that I am sorry he feels bitter he did not get the chance to come to America, but he was needed more at home. It upsets me to hear that he drinks so much and does not help Father with the work around the farm. Please tell him not to drink whiskey, for it makes him cross and that's no help to Father. The farm needs a strong young man's hand, and that is Brian's place.

America is a fine place, full of excitement, but if I could switch with Brian I would. Well, it would be a harder decision if Peter stayed here, but I do so long to see you all again! It's best that I came, though, for there are more jobs over here for Irish women than men.

I miss you all terribly, and I count the days till I can come back. Mary always said I should settle down with a good man and stay here, and that Peter Morley would make a fine husband. It causes me heartache to think of this mess I'm in, for I can't imagine leaving him, but yet I must in a few more years.

Peter is a fine man and he makes me laugh, but I must come back to Skibbereen, because the family needs me. Peter says he'll never go back to Ireland, so I doubt I'll ever be wed to him. It's a fine mess to be in, isn't it?

Dear Theresa, I must go. It is late and I am sitting here writing this letter when I should be sleeping. I get up early each morning to start the fire in the kitchen, and my day is a long one.

Please give my love to everyone at home, and pray for me. I need all of your prayers more than ever.

Love,

Rose

CHAPTER TEN

December 1887

It was a week before Christmas when Rose received the letter from her sister Theresa that their mother had died. "Her fears got the best of her," Theresa's letter said. "She would spend days in the corner of the house with a blanket over her head, mumbling that she could hear a horse walking around the outside. We tried to calm her down, but nothing worked. We were watching her closely, but she got out one night and was away for two days before Brian found her in old man Cleary's field, sitting on the ground shivering with cold. She got sick after that and had a terrible fever for a day or two, then she was gone."

Rose was sitting on her bed reading the letter, and all of a sudden it felt like everything stopped. She had to read Theresa's words over and over before they made sense. Her mother was dead. It was like the Earth under her feet had turned to water, like the sun had become stuck in the sky.

All these years she had believed she would see her mother again. She knew her mother was sick in the mind, of course, but she thought her body was healthy. She had been through many trials, but had survived them all, and Rose thought she would continue to survive. It was impossible that she could die.

Her poor, mad mother. There had been something wrong with her always, as long as Rose could remember. Some difference in the way she saw things. She would cock her head as if she was listening to some strange music, and sometimes she would go into a trance as if she was seeing something that other people could not see.

It got worse with each passing year. It was especially bad when Rose turned 12, because that was the age when her mother had seen her own mother die of starvation in the Great Famine. When Rose turned 12, that was when her mother began roaming the fields and hills at night, like some spectral figure that could not rest. She would come back in the morning with twigs and grass in her hair, her eyes with a mad gleam in them, and talking of fairy rings and strange creatures she'd seen in the night.

It was then she started accusing Rose of being a changeling, a fairy child. It wasn't all the time; for long periods, everything would be fine with them. Then, however, Rose would wake up in the night to see her mother standing over her cot, her face lit up from the candle she was holding, her eyes burning with a mad gleam, muttering a Gaelic incantation designed to send the changeling back to the fairies, and bring her own child back.

For all her wild ways, however, what Rose always remembered was how tenderly her mother would brush her long auburn hair when she was a child, how she'd make up rhymes about Rose's beautiful hair, and the happy times when they'd run about playing games. Her mother had a childlike joy on her good days that would warm the coldest heart.

And now she was gone. Gone, gone, and Rose had not had a chance to say goodbye.

It was a terrible sadness, and coming as it did at Christmas time made it worse. Rose knew she was supposed to be glad at this season of the year, but there was no happiness in her soul.

The Lancasters loved Christmas, and they made quite a big show of it every year. Mr. Lancaster and Martin cut down a huge evergreen tree from the woods that surrounded their property, and they and Peter put it up by the main staircase just inside the front door, and then everyone decorated it with ribbons and bows and candles and strings of candy and sweet treats. There were wreaths and garland everywhere, and mistletoe hanging from the rafters. On Christmas Eve they had a large gathering of family and friends for a dinner of pheasant and duck, and Mr. Lancaster opened his finest wine, and Mrs. Lancaster got out her finest china. After dinner Mrs. Lancaster played the piano, and Peter was invited to sing, which he did with gusto. He sang many Christmas songs and then some traditional Irish songs, which brought a tear to Rose's eye. There was an ache in his voice that went right to Rose's heart, and it was too much for her to take. She had to dab at her eyes and then leave the room while he was singing.

Christmas morning they opened presents around the tree, and although Rose laughed and smiled at all the gaiety, she had a wound in her heart that felt like it was going to kill her.

Peter noticed this and he came up to her and said, "Rose, we have the rest of the day free, and I have the whale of an idea. Why don't we go ice skating?"

"I don't feel like it," Rose said.

"Why not? It will do you good to get out in the fresh air. It's a bracing fine day outside, and I know a pond in Fairmount Park that will be frozen solid. There's plenty of snow out there and Mr. Lancaster said we could take the two-person sleigh for a ride. Come on, my girl, we'll make a grand afternoon out of it. I've already asked Victoria if you could borrow her ice skates, and she said yes."

"But I've never been ice skating. I'll fall and break my neck."

"Not at all, Rose. I wouldn't let something like that happen to you. I'll be there holding you up, my darling girl."

He was so strong and had such charm, and Rose needed to lean on someone right now. She agreed, and they set off with the black mare named Midnight hitched to the sleigh. They were bundled under several woolen blankets, and it was truly lovely to glide along the snowy landscape, with the trees looking like ghostly figures in white and a gentle snow falling from the gray sky.

"Isn't it a sight?" Peter said. "Why, I never saw snow till I came to this country. There's one marvel after another in this place."

"Aye, it has its charms," Rose said. "But it will never replace Ireland in my heart."

"Sure and the Old Sod has its beauty," Peter said. "But this is the place for the new, my girl. It makes me so excited I get carried away."

He burst into "Beautiful Dreamer", the Stephen Foster song.

"Beautiful dreamer, wake unto me,
Starlight and dewdrops are waiting for thee;
Sounds of the rude world, heard in the day,
Lull'd by the moonlight have all pass'd away!
Beautiful dreamer, queen of my song,
List while I woo thee with soft melody;
Gone are the cares of life's busy throng,
Beautiful dreamer, awake unto me!
Beautiful dreamer, awake unto me!"

His high, clear tenor seemed to ring out in the muffled silence of the snowy landscape, and it brought aching sadness mixed with joy to Rose's heart. Her heart was broken at her mother's death, but there was also joy in being in the presence of this big, happy man.

Peter talked and sang incessantly, but after a while he fell silent and just let the horse plod on, its footsteps muffled in the cocoon of silence that surrounded them. They wound their way through the fields and forested areas down toward Fairmount Park. Here and there were houses with ribbons of blue-gray smoke coming from their chimneys, and children playing in the snow, but otherwise all was quiet, save for the sound of train whistles in the distance and the steady jingle of the bells on Midnight's harness.

When they reached the park there was more activity. Peter guided the sleigh to a large pond that was frozen over, with dozens of skaters gliding across it. He brought the sleigh to a halt by a wooden bench where people were putting on their skates, and he tied Midnight to a post nearby, then he helped Rose down.

"Look at that," Peter said, pointing to the glistening surface of the pond. "Have you ever seen such a glorious sight? Come on, my lass, let's get out there and have some fun."

They put on their skates and then wobbled over to the pond, and Rose's feet promptly went out from under her as soon as she stepped on the slippery ice. She pulled Peter down with her, and they landed in a heap on the smooth surface.

"Are you all right, Rose?" Peter said, looking at her as if she were a china doll that had fallen off a cabinet.

Rose smiled at him, and then they burst into laughter at this predicament.

"I told you I can't skate," Rose said, when she finally caught her breath. "I can't even stand up, it seems."

"Don't worry, Rose, I'll help you," Peter said. He struggled to his feet and held his arm out for Rose to take. She grabbed on to his arm, rose halfway to her feet, and then her legs splayed out and she went down again, pulling Peter on top of her this time. They laughed again, till Rose had to wipe the tears of laughter from her face.

"Faith, I don't know if I'll ever get up on my own two feet," she said. "I don't think I was made for this pastime, Peter."

"Nonsense, my girl," Peter said. "We'll have you up and gliding about like a Dutchman in no time. Let's try it again."

He got up and lifted Rose to her feet, and they made their way across the ice, with Rose wobbling all the way. She could hardly go two steps without starting to lose her balance, and it was all Peter could do to hold her up. They almost went down several times, which caused them to laugh even more.

Rose felt secure in Peter's strong arms, and it was such a relief to laugh after the sadness of the last several days. She took Peter's arm and smiled up at him. He was such a handsome man, with his square jaw and his black hair spilling out of his red wool cap, his face flushed from the cold. She saw the way other women looked at him, and she marveled once more that a man so fine looking would be interested in her.

They made their way around the pond as if they were drunk, Rose holding on to Peter for dear life, laughing every time she slipped and he trying to right them both as she tugged on his arm. After a while Rose's balance improved, and she managed to skate by herself for a few feet before grabbing for Peter's arm again.

When they came back around to the wooden bench, Rose said, "My legs feel like they have lead in them. I need to rest a bit. You go ahead, Peter."

She sat there and watched him glide and spin about, moving his big body with grace and precision.

He winked at her as he glided by with his hands clasped behind his back, looking as calm as if he were taking a stroll on the beach. She shook her head and said, "How did an Irishman like yourself learn how to do that?"

"Oh, there's lots of things you don't know about me," he said, launching himself into a spin with his arms pulled tight against his body. "I used to live near here, and when I saw the skaters my first winter in this country, I was mad to learn the art of it. I had a friend who taught me."

It was a jewel of an afternoon, like a scene from a Currier and Ives lithograph. The white snow and the pearl gray sky made the colors of the skaters stand out vividly. A red cap, a green scarf, any color was emphasized. Off to one side of the pond there was a man tending a fire in a steel drum, and he was roasting chestnuts in a pan, with a pot of apple cider warming over the fire. Peter went over and got cups of cider and a bag of chestnuts, and brought them back to her on the bench.

The hot cider warmed Rose all the way to her toes, and she leaned her head on Peter's shoulder, happiness like a warm glow spreading through her. If only she could stay like this, in this cloud of happiness with Peter's strong arms to lean on, and no worries about her duty to her family, no sadness about her mother's passing. It was a dream, a pleasant Christmas dream that she did not want to end.

There were so many troublesome thoughts at the edge of her mind, though. She was 23, an age when many Irish girls who came to America were married. Peter had not mentioned marriage once, and he seemed in no hurry to settle down. He talked of his plans and ideas for the future, how he could do great things in this country, how the freedom was intoxicating for a boy from Ireland, and it all seemed like such a beautiful vision.

There was no little house with a wife and children in that vision, though. Then again, was that what she wanted? She had always thought she would be going back to Ireland, though the thought of going back without Peter was troubling to her.

She pushed those thoughts out of her mind once more, as she had done many times in the past. It was too glorious an afternoon to think of troubling things. She would just enjoy this Christmas day, and try to think only of the happiness she felt right now.

After they finished their cider, Peter got Rose up again, and they took a few more spins around the pond. Gradually the afternoon turned colder as the sun moved lower in the sky. The man selling chestnuts put out his fire and packed up his pot and pan, stowing them in a wagon hitched nearby. The skaters left in pairs, pulling their coats tight around themselves against the icy fingers of the winter afternoon.

"Well, my girl, I think we'd better be getting back," Peter said. "The day is getting late, and they'll be expecting us at home."

He bundled Rose into the sleigh, and before they started off, he reached into the pocket of his coat and produced a shiny metal flask.

"Here, this will take the edge off the cold," he said, handing it to Rose.

"What's this you're giving me?" she said.

"Just a little something to warm your insides," he said. "The cider man has left, so you'll need something else to keep the cold off your bones."

Rose had drunk a glass of wine on special occasions at the Lancasters' home, but she had never had anything stronger. She disapproved of whiskey, since she had seen the damage it did to so many of her countrymen and women.

It was bitter, biting cold, though, and she knew they had a long drive back to the warm fires of the Lancasters' home. She opened the cap and took a long draught of the flask, and the fiery liquid burned all the way down her throat. She choked as it went down, and the taste was so strong it brought tears to her eyes.

"What in God's name is that?" she said, coughing.

"Just some good Irish whiskey from Tullamore," he said, as Midnight pulled the sleigh forward. "It's the very thing to keep you warm on a day like this."

After Rose got over the initial shock of the taste, she enjoyed the pleasantly warm feeling the whiskey gave her. She took another drink and then gave the flask back to Peter, who took a long swallow and then put the flask back in his pocket.

Rose leaned her head against Peter's side and let the warm feelings spread. She realized she was definitely in love with this man, and she was happy he'd come into her life.

To their right the eastern sky had turned a deep purple, and it was spreading upward with each step the horse took. Lights were coming on in the farmhouses dotting the countryside as they made their way up the long, gradual slope of the land toward Chestnut Hill. Rose was comfortably warm under the thick woolen blankets and she dozed against Peter's side. She did not know how long she slept, but suddenly she realized the sleigh had stopped and Peter was speaking to her.

"Now, look at that, my girl. Isn't that the prettiest sight you've ever seen?"

They were stopped on a bluff overlooking the countryside. The sky was clear and a full moon was out, casting a silver light on the scene below. Here and there ribbons of smoke curled up from farmhouse chimneys, and candles glowed in the windows. In the distance a silver ribbon of the Schuylkill River shimmered around a bend, and the brick factories and row houses of Philadelphia appeared on the other bank. There was a soft yellow glow from the gas lighting, and here and there the spires of a church reached skyward.

"Yes, it is beautiful," Rose said. "Like a beautiful painting."

"We're lucky people, Rose Sullivan," Peter said. "Lucky to be alive at a time like this."

And then he kissed her. He had kissed her at other times since he came to America, and his kisses always left her breathless and aroused. This time, however, there was something more. More urgency. Passion. A greater need than ever before.

It called out to something inside her, which matched its intensity, like a forest fire that suddenly leaps across a chasm and ignites a nearby stand of trees. He kindled a passion in her that was hard to control. Once again his lips awakened new depths in her that she had not known of before.

His tongue was insistent, and his breath was hot on her face. He caressed her hair with his fingers, and he murmured her name in a husky voice. "I need you, Rose," he whispered. "I need you now, under this beautiful moon."

It was a magical night, and Rose let herself fall under its influence. Suddenly all the sadness of her mother's passing was transformed into passion. She needed Peter Morley with an urgent intensity, and she kissed him back with a mounting, frenzied passion.

They were hidden under the blankets, but underneath Peter had lifted up Rose's long skirt and his hand was running up her leg, his touch like scalding ice. She moaned as he did so, shivering with excitement. She ran her fingers inside his shirt, along his thickly muscled back, and pulled him closer.

It was like a waking dream, and when she thought of it later it seemed like it happened to someone else. Surely that was not her, Rose Sullivan, who was calling out passionate words, who was panting, moaning, shuddering, arching her spine, and raking her fingernails down his back. She no longer felt the cold. Her clothes were torn open and her flesh was naked to the night air, but she felt hot, not cold. She wanted only to feel this man closer, closer, closer. He was everything she ever wanted, and more. He was like the sun, blotting out everything that came before.

Her heart was laid bare, her deepest thoughts and desires were revealed to him, and she did not care. There was no holding back; she told him everything of herself, every secret her heart held. He was a maestro of desire, building her to a peak and then moving away from it, ceaselessly back and forth, like the tides of an ocean. It seemed to last hours, she had no idea how long it lasted, but finally, when he brought her to a shuddering peak and she crossed over to the other side, it was like a great wave had washed over her and she was left thrown up on the shore, limp and drained of everything.

They lay together in an embrace and she looked past his shoulders, up at the moon and the stars, and she listened to the far off whistle of trains and the steam coming off the back of Midnight, the horse snorting as if it was impatient to get going again.

And Rose realized with a stunning certainty that she was carrying Peter's child now.

CHAPTER ELEVEN

When Peter thought about that night later it stood out in his mind like a picture, something beautiful and frozen, a tableau of a winter scene. You could have hung it on the wall of your parlor, and it would have been something to marvel at.

But it was not as permanent as a painting. It was more like a delicate snowflake, a beautiful sculpture in ice that melted away in a minute.

The window that opened into Rose's soul was shut immediately. She was still the shy, reserved girl from Skibbereen, and in fact she drew even further into herself.

After it was over, she put her clothes back on and wrapped the blankets around her more tightly than before, and she rode home with him in silence. He tried to make her laugh, but she would not even smile. He tried singing, for his voice had always had a good effect on women, but she merely stared off into the distance, her face a stony mask.

The priests, he thought. It was the priests, with their endless talk of sin and damnation, that was it. She was thinking they'd done something wrong, something he and she would burn in Hell for. He'd seen it before in the old country, when girls would suddenly talk about going to Confession after kissing him, as if they'd done something terribly wrong.

Or was it something else? He had seen the way Martin Lancaster acted around her. He had heard the hushed voices and the furtive looks. She told him that she had no feelings for Martin, but how was he to know if that was true? A rich young man like Martin Lancaster would be a fine catch for a poor Irish lass like Rose. Martin's family would disown him if he was ever so foolish as to marry Rose, but he was a man of education and breeding and he'd land on his feet, surely.

And what have I to offer her? Peter thought. I'm a driver of horses, a coachman. I have no education, no breeding. I'm a poor Irishman who can't offer her much more than she had in the old country. Compared to Martin Lancaster I'm a nothing, a nobody.

He lapsed into silence as he drove the sleigh, the only sound the jingling of the horse's harness and the hissing of the sleigh's runners on the snowy road. When they reached home Peter helped Rose down from the sleigh, and she stood up on her toes and gave him a quick kiss, then scurried into the house. He took the sleigh back to the barn and unhitched Midnight, then fed and groomed her, his thoughts scattered and tinged with sadness.

He watched and waited, hoping that she'd warm up again, but in the weeks to come she avoided him. She would be polite whenever he was around, but she never smiled, and she seemed not to want him to touch her. She seemed warmer around Martin, but maybe that was simply the actions of a servant who did not want to anger her master.

It was all so puzzling. Peter decided that he did not understand women at all. They were strange, wonderful, magical creatures, but there was "no figuring them", as Murphy used to say.

A month passed, and one day he came upon her in the kitchen vomiting into the cast iron sink.

"Are you all right?" he said, touching her tenderly on the shoulder.

"I don't know what's wrong with me," she gasped. "I was cooking the eggs for breakfast, but just looking at them made me sick."

Later that week she took to her bed, and when she got up several days later she looked shaky and pale. There were hushed conversations among the women of the house, conversations that would suddenly stop when Peter came into the room.

Then one evening Mrs. Lancaster summoned Peter to the parlor, and when he arrived he found Mr. Lancaster sitting next to her with a look on his face as if he was having problems with his digestion.

"Sit down, Peter," Mr. Lancaster said. "There is something we need to, ah, talk to you about." Mrs. Lancaster's lips were pursed, and her eyes were narrowed in disapproval at Peter.

He sat down in the nearest chair, feeling like his body was too big, his legs too long, for the delicate walnut chair with its red cushions. He did not know what to do with his hands, so he clenched them tightly in his lap.

"Something you need to talk to me about?" Peter said. "And what could that be, Your Honor?"

"This is a difficult subject to broach," Mr. Lancaster said. He fidgeted in his chair, but at a stern glance from his wife he continued. "It has come to our attention that, uh. . ." his voice trailed off and he looked at the ceiling.

"Henry!" Mrs. Lancaster said. "Please continue."

"Yes, yes," Mr. Lancaster said. "Peter, it seems that Rose is expecting a child."

"A child?" Peter said. "I don't understand, Your Honor. Did you say a child?"

"Yes he did," Mrs. Lancaster said. "A child. Do you have anything to say, Peter?"

Peter sat there smiling at them, unable to speak. The only sound was the ticking of the grandfather clock in the hallway. Otherwise, the house was strangely silent.

Finally, Peter found speech. "I don't know exactly what to say," he offered. "Are you sure about this?"

"It is certain," Mrs. Lancaster snapped. "The girl is expecting a child."

"I see," Peter said.

"Without the blessing of holy matrimony, I might add," Mrs. Lancaster said.

Peter smiled again. He ardently wished that he could somehow disappear, that he could rub a magic stone in his pocket and become invisible, like some of the stories he had heard from Murphy about fairies and witches and magical stones. But that was back in Ireland, and none of that magic would work here, he knew.

"Peter, we know that you have been something of an, ah, suitor of Rose's," Mr. Lancaster said. He seemed as uncomfortable as Peter, and probably wished he could disappear also. "Is that not correct?"

"I have had a fancy for the girl, it's true," Peter said. "She is a pretty Irish lass."

"Well, ah, what I am driving at. . ." Mr. Lancaster said, fumbling again for words.

"What he means is, are you prepared to marry her?" Mrs. Lancaster interrupted.

Peter was thunderstruck. It was a moment before he could speak. "Marry? Why, I don't think we ever discussed such a prospect. No, I don't think Rose and I have ever got to that point."

"No?" Mrs. Lancaster said. "Well, you might have discussed it before you. . . before you took advantage of her in such a fashion!" Her face was red with emotion, and her eyes were flashing. "Really, Peter, I am appalled at you! To take advantage of a young girl like Rose in that manner. I thought you were a good Christian man. Apparently, I was wrong. Henry, you know what to say, don't you?"

Her husband cleared his throat, shifted in his chair, and said: "Peter, as Mrs. Lancaster said, we expected better of you. However, be that as it may, I assume you are going to do the honorable thing and marry young Rose. If so, you may stay in our employ. Rose, of course, will have to be dismissed. She will not be able to perform her duties while she is carrying the child, and afterward, well, we are not prepared to have a housemaid living here with an infant."

He paused.

"You know that is not all of it, Henry," Mrs. Lancaster said. "Please continue."

"Yes, dear," her husband said. "Ah, if you decide not to marry Rose, Peter, both of you will be dismissed immediately. We can not condone such immorality among our domestic staff. I will not be able to give you a reference, of course, which means that you will not be able to find work as a coachman in this country ever again."

The air in the room felt very close all of a sudden. Peter pulled at his collar, and realized he was sweating. He felt like a trapped animal. Marry Rose! That had not been his plan at all. She was a lovely young girl, and it was true that he cared for her, but she had been plain with him about her desire to return to Ireland. There was no returning to the old country for him.

On the other hand, he did not fancy the prospect of leaving this big, comfortable house and going back to a life of digging ditches and living in a rooming house crowded with Irish immigrants in Philadelphia.

There was no way out. He had to stay here. This is where Peter Morley would make his life. He could not, would not, take one step backward.

"What is your decision?" Mrs. Lancaster said. She was eyeing him coldly, rather like the Pope sizing up a heretic, and it was clear she would have no pity on him.

"Why, of course I'll marry Rose," Peter said, smiling weakly. "I can't think of anything else I'd rather do."

"Splendid!" Mr. Lancaster said, a smile of relief crossing his face. "Happy to hear it. That's good news, isn't it dear?"

Mrs. Lancaster smiled, although her eyes were still narrowed and she seemed suspicious. "I suppose it is," she said. "When will you be married?"

"Oh, I'll have to talk to Rose about that," Peter said. "I suppose we'll want to do it as soon as we can. We'll talk to the parish priest about it, and find out how soon he can fit us in."

"Capital idea," Mr. Lancaster said. "Well, we're finished here, aren't we dear? Rose will have to leave, as we said, but since you're going to be the sole support for her and the child, Peter, I will increase your wages to seven dollars a week. That should be adequate." He sat back in his chair, beaming, waiting for approval for his beneficence.

"Thank you, Your Honor," Peter said, on cue. "You're a generous man, to be sure. Rose and I appreciate it, we do."

That night, alone in his bed in the basement, was the first time Peter thought of running away.

CHAPTER TWELVE

December 1888

Dear Father, Brian, Theresa, and Annie,

I cannot tell you how sad it made me to read Theresa's letter last week, the one she wrote for Father. I have been crying for days, and I am hardly able to put pen to paper now without getting the letter wet with my tears.

I have lived here for eight years, and my only thought during all that time was of my family at home. I saved my money and sent home as much as I could, and I prayed for you all each night, and thought of you every minute of every day. I never intended to stay in this country like other girls, never wanted to find a man and settle down. My only thought was to come back to my home once again.

It was a terrible thing to read a letter from my own sister, with my father's words telling me I could never come home again because I brought shame on the family. Yes it is true that I have a baby now, but I am a married woman. Yes it is true that I was in a family way before I got married, but I think it was a mean, spiteful thing for Mary Driscoll to write and tell you what happened to me. She has never forgiven me for not supporting her when she was caught stealing, and now she has taken her revenge. You must not believe all the lies that Mary has told you, I beg of you.

For it is a fact that the father of my child, a man named Peter Morley, has married me. You may remember that I wrote about him before. I met him the night before I left Ireland, and after many a year he turned up in the employ of the family I worked for in Philadelphia, which I think was God's Will. He's a fine, strong man, and he is full of spirit, and he'll make a good husband. I knew from the moment I met him that I loved him, and perhaps I let my feelings get the better of me. We had our gaieties, our moments of Love's embrace, and the result is next to me in a cradle as I write these words: my darling son Timothy.

He is a beautiful boy, with his father's smile and my eyes. He has a ruddy complexion like our Father, Theresa, and he seems a peaceful soul, lying for hours in my arms without a sound, just looking up at me with his deep questioning eyes.

How I would love for you to see him! I want my darling boy to see his family, to walk the fields of dear old Skibbereen the way I did as a girl. He will grow to be a fine, strong man, of this I am sure, and I want him to be part of the family, our family, that goes back through the generations. So many people in this country are cut off from their roots, and I meet many Irish girls who have no intention of ever going back to their homeland. I do not want that for my son.

It saddens me that even Peter, my husband, has no feeling for his homeland. When we first got married I told him I wanted to move back to Ireland, but he refused. He wants no part of "sleepy old Eire" as he calls it. He thinks that America is the land of promise and excitement for a young man, and he wants to be part of it. I had thought that I could persuade him in time to go back to Ireland with Timothy and me, but now that prospect is closed forever since your letter came.

Theresa, I beg of you to ask Father to reconsider his decision. The thought of never seeing my family again makes me feel as if my right arm has been cut off. I would almost rather have never walked up the gangplank onto the ship that brought me here, than to have this happen. And yet, if I had not come here I would never have had this beautiful baby.

It is hard to be judged for what I have done. I have not set foot in a church in months, because one of the local gossips told the priest at our parish about my condition, and he would not marry Peter and me. Praise God, we at least got our marriage certificate from the government, but it pains me to be cut off from my church, and I worry that I can not get Timothy baptized. It does not bother Peter, for he was never a man with much religious feeling, but it makes my heart ache. I sometimes have a dream that I am back in Skibbereen where no one knows my shame, and everyone treats me like the girl I used to be.

I know it's a dream, but do you think Father will ever reconsider his decision? Think of how I could help you on the farm! Father is getting older, as you said, and he is in constant pain from his rheumatism. It seems that Brian is not much help, spending so much of his time drinking and carousing. If I came home I could help you and Annie with the work, and relieve Father of some of his burden. I have worked very hard in my years in America, and I know how to do just about everything involved with running a house, including cooking, cleaning, washing, and many other things. I am not afraid of hard work.

I have no work at the moment because my employer, Mrs. Lancaster, dismissed me from service when she discovered my situation. The wealthy women here will not hire a girl who has had a baby, so I can find no other employment. Peter is supporting us on his wages as a coachman at the Lancasters' home, but it is hard to make ends meet. It can be lonely sometimes, too, because Peter is still required to sleep in the Lancasters' house most nights, only staying with me a night or two each week. I live in a small room in a boarding house in West Philadelphia, and it is so crowded and cramped here that I long for the open spaces of Cork again. The house is surrounded by many other houses, and hundreds of people live in a small area. The walls are thin, and my neighbors argue and shout all night long, which makes sleeping difficult for the baby and me. It is much colder here in the winter than at home, and we can not afford to keep our room heated all night long -- I must let the coal fire die out and then restart it in the morning, and the air is so cold that I shiver as I am doing it.

I do not like to complain, and I try to keep my spirits up, but this is not the life I imagined for myself. I don't think Peter likes to come here, and I can hardly blame him. Most of the week he lives in a room in a grand house in Chestnut Hill, eats good meals with the other servants, and gets to dress up in his fine coachman's uniform and drive a beautiful carriage all over the city. To come here and sleep in this cold, cramped room and eat the plain fare we partake of is a hardship to him.

Peter has big dreams, and the way his face lights up when he talks of them, I have no doubt they will come true. He tells me that when he is driving the carriage for Mr. Lancaster they talk about all the inventions that seem to be appearing almost daily, and how they will change our lives. There is a man named Thomas Edison who works near here in New Jersey, and he is a marvel, inventing all sorts of new mechanical devices. You may know that he has invented an electrical light that is replacing gaslight everywhere over here. He has many other inventions too, including a machine that records music and plays it back, and now Peter says Mr. Lancaster told him

*that Edison has invented something even more marvelous --
something called a motion picture camera, that takes pictures of
people moving about in real life, and those pictures can be played
back. Peter says Mr. Lancaster thinks this will be Edison's greatest
invention, and that it will replace music halls and vaudeville shows.*

*I told you before that Peter has the most beautiful singing
voice, and he tells me that he dreams of being on the stage some day.
He sings Irish songs at the Lancasters' parties, and everyone
remarks on the sweet, angelic tone he has. It is hard for an Irishman
to get work in the theater here, however. There are comedians who
dress up as the Irish and talk in brogues here, but it is all to make
fun of us. Peter thinks that some day there may be opportunities for
him on the stage, and he is biding his time.*

*I must finish my letter, because Baby Timothy is getting
restless, and needs to be fed. I implore you once again, Theresa, to
ask Father to reconsider. I know he must be ashamed of me after you
read Mary Driscoll's letter to him, and I am sorry for having
brought this disgrace to him. I would not undo what I did, though,
because I have a beautiful, precious baby as the result. Please tell
Father to forgive me, and think of the grandson he has here in
America. I would like nothing better than to bring Timothy over to
see his homeland in a year or two. Perhaps it is just a dream -- I
could not afford a ticket on the ship if it were today -- but I need this
dream to sustain me in these hard times. I cannot bear the thought of
never seeing my family again.*

*I think of you all before I sleep at night, and I pray for every
one of you. I pray that Father's body will not ache so much, that
Brian will stop his drinking, and that you and Annie will find
happiness and love in our fair country. I have no money to send you
now, but I hope some day to send money once again.*

Please pray for me.
Your loving sister,

Rose

CHAPTER THIRTEEN

June 1893

"Mama, I don't want to get my picture taken," Tim said. "It's hot in these shoes and I want to take them off."

They were sitting in a photographer's studio on Market Street in Philadelphia, Rose and her two boys, Tim and Paul. Tim was five years old, and Paul was two. They were wearing blue sailor suits, with short pants and high black leather shoes. They usually went barefoot in the summer, and neither one liked the confinement of the black leather shoes.

Rose had on a long blue dress buttoned all the way up to the neck, and a wide-brimmed hat. It was a stylish outfit, as were the sailor suits, and they cost her so much that she could not afford the street car fare to the photography studio, and had to walk the 40 blocks from her room at the edge of West Philadelphia. She pushed Paul in a carriage, but Tim had to walk, and he complained mightily about it. Every so often she would lift Paul out of the carriage and let Tim get in, and she'd carry Paul and push Tim for a few blocks.

The price for the photographic portrait would mean that she could not eat meat for several weeks, and the boys would complain about eating oatmeal three times a day.

It was a sacrifice, but she was prepared to make it, for she planned to send this photograph to Theresa at home, to show the family how well she was doing in America. Her two beautiful boys in their sailor suits, and she in her fine dress, would be proof that all was well for Rose Sullivan McCarthy.

She hoped they would not ask why her husband was not in the picture.

Peter had left a week before, to drive the carriage to the Lancasters' summer home in Maine. The family would be there till late August, and if Rose was lucky Peter might be allowed to come home on the train for a brief weekend visit sometime in July. The Lancasters had bought the property in Maine three years ago, and so this was the third summer that Peter had been away from Rose.

"Madam, can you please ask your sons to settle down and pose the way I asked?" the photographer said once again. He was a bossy little man with a fuzzy brown mustache, and he seemed anxious to get the session over with. Rose resettled Paul on her lap, and posed Tim once again next to her chair, telling him to "stand up straight like a little man and make your father proud".

Whether Peter really was proud of his sons was another matter. He seemed strangely aloof from them for a man who was known for his friendly, spirited personality. He lapsed into long silences when he was home, and did not seem interested in talking to his boys, the way Rose thought a father should.

"Madam, your boy is not paying attention," the photographer said, pointing at Tim. "Can you please get him to look at the camera?". He had been waving a metal toy soldier in the air to get the boys to look at him, but Tim had his head buried in his mother's lap and was stubbornly ignoring him.

"Stand up straight and put on a serious face for the nice man, Tim," Rose said. "It's only a little longer you'll have to do this, I promise."

Tim gave a huge sigh, but he straightened up and stared into the camera lens. The photographer ducked his head behind the big black box and then there was a blinding flash and the smell of phosphate. Tim rubbed his eyes and Paul squalled in fright, his round body a tense little ball in Rose's lap.

"The baby moved again," the photographer said, pursing his lips. "We'll have to take at least one more."

"Hush, boys," Rose said. "It's not much longer. Mama will buy you some ice cream if you behave."

Ice cream was a luxury she could not afford. She had only a few pennies left in her purse after paying the photographer, and they could definitely be used for other things. But she wanted this picture so badly, wanted her sons to look as handsome as possible, and she was not above bribing them with the promise of a treat.

She would get two copies of the picture. One she would send to her sister Theresa in Ireland, but the other she would hang in her room at the boarding house. She hoped that the picture of the boys would fill Peter with pride when he saw it, the pride of a father in his sons, and that maybe it would soften his heart towards them.

What had happened to her marriage? She lay in bed sometimes at night and tried to find the answer to that question. When Peter came to her five years ago and asked her to marry him there had been an edge in his voice, something different from the laughing, light-hearted voice of the man she knew. He had married her quickly, in a hurried ceremony at City Hall in Philadelphia, with a friend of his named Patrick and the Lancasters' other housemaid Tessie as their witnesses. They took a two-day trip to the seaside at Cape May, New Jersey, to consummate their marriage, and then she moved into the room he had rented in West Philadelphia, far from the grand homes of Chestnut Hill where the Lancasters lived.

It had been hard to adjust to this new phase of her life. She was sick many days while she was carrying Tim, for one thing. And the noisy, crowded section of the city where she lived was so different than the palatial home and spacious grounds of the Lancasters. Peter spent most of his time away, and she was alone a lot. She dreamed of her home, her family, her life in Ireland. It had always been her one hope to go back.

She thought the sadness was gone when Tim was born, though. He was born in her bed, and when the midwife gave him to her, she cried tears of joy. He was so perfect, such a tiny miracle in her arms, and she could not believe how lucky she was to have him.

Her joy turned to ashes a month later, when the letter from Theresa arrived. "Father says you have disgraced us," it said. "You have brought shame on the family. He told me to write and tell you never to come back to Skibbereen, that you are not welcome here."

The words were like a knife to her heart. She held the letter in her trembling hand and reread the sentences over and over, not believing them. "Mary Driscoll wrote and told us what you have done," the letter said.

Mary Driscoll. She had written to them and spewed the gossip she'd heard through the network of Irish immigrants in Philadelphia. The world was somehow smaller and meaner than Rose had ever thought. The news of her shame had traveled across the sea as easily as if her family had lived across the street.

It was crushing, and she could not live with the finality of it. It had been thirteen years since she left them, but always she had thought she would go back. She knew well enough there was no money to buy a steamship ticket now, but she had always dreamed of the day when she could.

She could not accept it, so she never stopped writing to them. She wrote constantly, although it took Theresa longer and longer to reply. It was as if the bonds were slowly fraying, and Rose was trying desperately to hang on.

This portrait would help, she believed. They would all see their young relatives. Father would see his first grandchildren, and his heart would soften. Surely that would happen, would it not? Theresa and Annie and Brian would fall in love with their little nephews. Perhaps they would find a way to come and visit, or maybe stay in America with her. In her daydreams she would imagine them all living in the same house, just like in Skibbereen, and everything would be as it was when she was a little girl. Perhaps they would buy a small farm in New Jersey, and they could start a new life here. It would salve her loneliness to have her family nearby.

The photographer took another picture and then pronounced himself finished, instructing Rose to come back in two weeks to pick up her prints. Rose gathered her two boys together and started back down Market Street. Outside, the streets were crowded with activity: business people, pushcarts, carriages, streetcars, wagons, policemen on horses. Everywhere was the noise and urgency of humanity. Where are they all going? she wondered. When she was in the midst of all this energy and noise she felt so much like the country girl from County Cork, bewildered by it all.

She sometimes wondered what her mother would think of Philadelphia. She'd probably be afraid of all the noise and the crowds. She'd have that look in her eyes like she was seeing things other people could not perceive, and she'd be mumbling to herself about the Good People.

And where were they, the Good People? Were they here in America? It seemed there was no room in this crowded, busy place for the Good People and the other races of spirits who lived in Ireland. There was no history here, no myth or legend in this bustling, impatient country, and the spirits had no power in this part of the world.

And yet she still heard the clop-clop of horses' hooves sometimes, late at night, in her dreams. I am only half here, she often thought, and half in the country of my birth.

She had promised the boys a treat, so she stopped at an ice cream parlor and bought scoops of vanilla and chocolate ice cream in paper shells, and they sat at a marble-topped table outside and watched the panorama of the city passing by. Across the street was a theater, The Corinthian, a large brick building with white columns out front, and there were signs advertising a vaudeville show, with two "Irish" comedians named Clancy and O'Toole on the bill. Rose had never been to a vaudeville show, although she had heard that these comedians were not Irish at all, but men of "good, Protestant, American stock", as they were called, who dressed up in battered top hats and swallowtail coats with holes in the elbows, and told stories in thick brogues that made fun of the Irish. They were wildly popular, and even genteel people like the Lancasters had gone to see them. How could Peter ever feel at home, she wondered, in a country that produced Clancy and O'Toole?

"Mama, why doesn't Father live with us?" Tim said. He had chocolate ice cream dripping down his face, and Rose took a napkin and wiped his mouth with it. He had such an innocent, open manner, and he often asked questions that were so simple and direct they made Rose pause.

"I've told you before, darling boy," Rose said. "Father works for a rich family and they go to a place called Maine every summer. He is required to live with them, and it is far away from here. He wishes he could be with us, but he must wait till the family comes back in August. He writes us letters, remember? We must listen for his voice in those letters."

"Francis Mangan says my father is a scoundrel," Tim said. "He said his mother told him that."

Rose sighed. It was Mary Driscoll again. She had spread the news in the Irish community that Rose and Peter were not married when Tim was conceived, and this followed Rose around like a black cloud. She never knew when she met someone whether they knew the story or not, but now it was clear that women were telling their children, and poor little Tim was going to have to hear it, probably many times in his childhood.

"Of course you have a father," Rose said, wiping Tim's face again. "Don't believe that nasty little Francis Mangan. Your father drives a great big coach for a grand family. The man he works for is very important: he is one of the top men in charge of the railroad, and he does marvelous important things. Remember, Father wrote to us about how the Lancasters stopped in Massachusetts on the way to Maine, and they visited a company that makes motor cars? Father says these cars will be the newest thing, and soon the cities will be full of them. Mr. Lancaster knows about these matters, and he and Father discuss all the latest inventions and developments. Father says Mr. Lancaster thinks he's a smart man, bright as a new penny. Mr. Lancaster says Father is the smartest coachman he's ever had."

"Tell me again about how Father dresses," Tim said.

"Why, he dresses in a grand black uniform with a cap and gloves. He cuts a fine figure, and people remark every day about how handsome he looks."

Tim thought it over. "I've never seen him dressed like that."

"That's because he's not at work when he comes to see us," Rose said. "He only wears his uniform when he's working, silly boy. Now, that's enough talk about Father. Finish your ice cream so we can get started home."

They walked home amid the lengthening rays of the late afternoon sun slanting through the spaces between the tall brick buildings, and Rose carried Paul, now asleep on her shoulder, while she pushed Tim in the carriage. She saw the tall white spire of a church across the street, and she felt a pull towards it. She had not been inside a church in months, afraid of the disapproving stares of the Irish women she would encounter.

She crossed the street and went over to the gray stone building with the steep marble steps leading up to large red wooden doors. A wooden sign next to the stairs said, "St. Paul's Episcopal Church". She had never been inside a Protestant church before, but she needed to talk to God, and she decided He would just as soon be inside this place as any other church. She parked the carriage and got Tim out, saying, "Come on, Tim, we're going to stop here for a moment." Paul was still asleep on her shoulder as she led Tim up the steps.

Tim started to protest, but when she took him up the steps and into the church, he got quiet as soon as they entered the hushed, darkened sanctuary. There was a long narrow aisle with burnished wooden pews on either side of it, and a rainbow of sunlight streamed in from stained glass windows above the altar. The church was empty, it seemed, and Rose made her way slowly up the aisle to the pew nearest the altar, which was a simple affair, just a polished walnut table with some flowers on it and a gold cross. There were no statues of saints or the Virgin, no crucified Jesus hanging ten feet in the air behind the altar, no candles or incense burning.

Paul woke up and rubbed his eyes as Rose knelt down in the pew, but he did not make a sound. Both boys seemed awed by the silence around them. Rose looked up at the stained glass window, which portrayed Jesus in the Garden of Gethsemane, and she tried to pray. She started to say a Hail Mary, but the words would not come.

Is it because I am in a Protestant church? Why, my father would be shocked if he could see me now. He would probably thunder something about me going to Hell for setting foot inside this place.

She decided to simply talk to God in her own words.

Dear Lord, I feel that I am sinking. I do not know what to do; please help me. Peter is not the same man I knew, my family has disowned me, I have these two little boys and I have no money. Sometimes I feel that I cannot go on. What will I do? I have no place in this country, but I cannot go home again. Time is moving on and I cannot stop it. Sometimes I wish I could go back to before Time speeded up, back to a former day when I could change the decisions I made. That cannot be, I know. I cannot fight the flow of Time, just like I cannot stop the flow of the River Lee in my homeland. Help me, Lord.

She bowed her head and blinked her eyes, trying to hide her tears from the boys.

"And what have we here?"

Rose turned to see a priest, or whatever the Episcopals called their holy men, standing next to her, with his hands folded across his chest. He wore a plain gray suit with a white collar, and he had snow-white hair and sky blue eyes.

"I just stopped in to say a prayer," Rose said.

"The church is closed, my child," the priest said. "You'll have to come back tomorrow."

"But I can't come back tomorrow," Rose said. "I live miles from here, and I'd have to walk these two small boys back, and I need to speak to God now about my situation. I have no money, Father, and I'm desperate."

"Desperate?" the priest said. "Really? You have quite a fine dress on, I see. And those two young rascals with you are dressed like little princes. Why, you look like a very fine class of people to me."

"I used my last few dollars to buy these clothes," Rose said. "I just wanted my father in Ireland to see his grandchildren. I wanted a picture to show him, to show him that his daughter dresses like a grand lady, you see. I'm sure he's worried about me, even though he won't say it because I. . . well, because he has. . . you see, a vicious woman has written to him and told him terrible things about me. I have these children, you see, and. . ." The words poured out in a torrent and Rose could not straighten them out, could not get them to make sense. She did not know how to arrange the words into a logical story. She kept trying to start over, to tell the story from the beginning, but she couldn't get it to make sense.

The priest put his hand on her shoulder and smiled. "I think I understand," he said. "Would you like a meal? I was just getting ready to sit down for my supper. I'm sure my wife could set a few extra places at the table. I would be delighted if you and your children would join us."

Rose tried to answer, but her throat choked up and she began to cry.

CHAPTER FOURTEEN

There were times when Peter woke up at night covered with sweat, with a feeling that something large and heavy was leaning on his chest, a Presence, some type of beast with foul breath and gleaming red eyes. He struggled to cry out, but all that came was a strangled moan, and he'd thrash about in the bed till finally he awoke, gasping for breath, his heart pumping like it was about to break through the wall of his chest.

When this happened with Rose she would try to comfort him, to hold him and soothe him until he fell asleep again. When he was alone in bed in the Lancasters' house, it took him a long time to settle down and go back to sleep.

He knew what was attacking him in his dreams. It was the unquiet spirit of the Lieutenant he'd killed. It was a vengeful thing that wanted justice for his crime, and it was trying to pull him into the netherworld, where it would have its way with him.

In the daytime Peter could forget about what he'd done, but in the middle of the night he could not escape. The fear came back and sat on his chest, suffocating him with its weight.

He knew he should go to Confession and tell his sins to a priest, but he could not bring himself to do it. "You must make restitution," the priest would say, but Peter could never do that.

Instead, he struggled through the nights and kept things light and happy in the daytime, pushing the dark thoughts out of his mind with jokes and conversation.

And women.

Peter loved women, and he learned how to tell when women were interested in him. They got a certain light in their eyes, they looked at him differently. It was a small thing, and he doubted if other men could tell.

But he could. He knew by the way the air in a room seemed charged with electricity when a woman looked at him. It was a wordless, unspoken thing but it was like a current was passing between them, and it made his skin tingle and his breath come short.

And now Victoria Lancaster was looking at him that way.

Victoria had cast off the timidity of her youth and grown into a beautiful, confident young woman with blonde wavy hair and crystal blue eyes, and she had many suitors. She had been to finishing school but she resisted her parents' attempts to marry her off to some stuffy young man from one of Philadelphia's Society families. She considered herself a modern woman and she wanted to experience the world before she settled down to a life of raising the next generation of Lancasters. She studied Art, and she was interested in all the latest inventions. She had a typewriter, and she wrote stories on it, some of which were published in women's magazines.

Victoria played the piano like her mother, and when she heard Peter's high Irish tenor, she marveled at it. "You have such a special voice," she told him, "and the world needs to hear it."

She would often coax Peter into sitting down next to her at the piano, and she would accompany him while he sang popular songs. At the Lancasters' dinner parties she insisted that he sing with her, and he enjoyed it immensely, the men and women looking at him with rapt attention while he sang and Victoria played the piano next to him.

Peter could tell that she found him handsome. He loved to stand near her at the piano and watch the way her long, graceful fingers ran along the keys, the way her back arched when she played, the way her blonde hair curled down over her creamy white neck. He had to marvel at his good fortune at times like this.

I've come a long way from Tullamore, he would think.

It was madness to think that anything could happen with Victoria, of course. She was of a vastly different station than himself. He knew from his childhood that there was a wall separating the rich from people of his kind.

There was also the fact that he was married, with two young children.

The marriage. In the lonely hours in the middle of the night he had already admitted to himself that it was a sham. The wedding had been a hasty thing, and he had never quite reconciled himself to the fact of being married. Rose was a lovely girl, but he had never thought of settling down with her or anyone else, at least not at this point in his life.

Then there was the other problem.

He had always wondered about Tim, the oldest boy. He had seen the way Martin Lancaster looked at Rose, how he acted around her, and he could not get the thought out of his mind that the boy might really be Martin's.

It was not something he'd ever said to Rose, but it was always there, in the back of his mind. Martin had never married, and he often asked Peter how Rose was doing. He seemed to care deeply about her even now, five years after Rose had left the Lancasters' employ. It was obvious he still had feelings for her.

The times when Martin asked about Rose, Peter would smile and say, "The girl's as happy as happy can be," but he knew that was a lie. Rose did not like the long periods when Peter was away, and his brief visits home only made the pain more acute for her. When Peter came home it was one thing after another: they argued about money, the boys would pester Peter for his attention, the rooming house was always hot and smelly in summer and cold in the winter. There were so many immigrant Irish drinking and carousing and arguing all night long that it gave Peter a headache, and that always put him in a sour mood.

Then there were the times when being around a young, pretty lass like Victoria made Peter hungry for the touch of a woman, the feel of a woman's skin on his, and the sweet kisses that would blunt the rage, terror, and sadness he carried around inside him.

Sometimes, when he felt the fire burning fiercely inside him, he could still find satisfaction with Rose. At those times he would go to Rose and they would once again exult in each other's bodies, and slake their passion. It was never the same as that wintry Christmas night in the sleigh so long ago, though. Now it was a quick, furtive thing, hidden under blankets and with their voices muffled so they would not wake the little boys sleeping in a corner of the room.

It was such a night that had produced Paul, and although Peter was happy to see the tiny serious face blinking up at him when Paul was born, he was also filled with anxiety over the prospect of another mouth to feed. He stayed away for three weeks after Paul's birth, telling the Lancasters that Rose had gone to visit a sister in Boston and that was why he was not going home to her.

He felt a terrible guilt about that, but he pushed it out of his mind, just like he pushed anything unpleasant out. It was the only way he could go on.

Things were easier in the summers, when he was in Maine. Instead of the hot, noisy rooming house or the tiny bedroom in the basement he was living in a servant's cabin next to the Lancasters' grand mansion on a lake, and the cool breezes and placid water were a balm to his soul. He spent a lot of time outdoors with the family, and at nights when they entertained their friends who lived nearby, Peter got to sing at the piano with Victoria. There was much laughter and song and the nights were sparkling, luminous affairs with torches on the beach that reflected off the lake, and a fireworks display on the Fourth of July.

In the summer of 1893 Victoria found a new hobby, photography. She bought a large black Kodak box camera and a tripod, and she went out every day on photographic excursions. She often asked Peter to take her out in the carriage to some remote spot where the light was just right, and he began to look forward to these times alone with her.

One time they were on the beach of Snowy Egret Lake, where Victoria had the camera set up to take a picture of an abandoned wooden rowboat against the backdrop of the water. The faded, chipped white boat was striking against the clear blue sky and tea colored lake water. The sun was hot, and Peter was dressed in a white long sleeved shirt and black pants, with black leather shoes. Victoria had on a long sleeved white blouse buttoned up to the neck and a long blue skirt, her hair pulled back in a bun.

They had parked the carriage half a mile away and Peter carried the heavy camera through a thickly forested area to get to this beach. He was sweating in his shirt, and the mosquitoes were biting him on every inch of exposed skin.

"How much longer will this take?" he said to Victoria. "The mosquitoes here seem to like the taste of an Irishman."

"Not much longer," Victoria said, fussing over her camera. "I just want to get a few good pictures."

"I don't understand why these confounded creatures seem to only be attacking me," Peter said, swatting at another mosquito.

"I've been told they're attracted to sweetness," Victoria said, laughing. "I believe you must be a sweeter person than me, Peter."

"Thank you, Miss Victoria," Peter said. "But you're being too modest. You're the sweetest person in the State of Maine, I do believe."

"You won't say that when you hear what I've been thinking," Victoria said. "I have an idea that I'd like to take a picture of you by that boat. But you have to stand completely still, no matter how many times you get bitten."

"Sure and that would be torture," Peter said. "Why, those nasty little creatures would have the time of their lives, taking pieces out of me."

"Oh, but it would make such a good picture," Victoria pleaded. "Won't you do it, please? The light is perfect, and I am sure the contrast between the white boat and your black hair would be thrilling." She smiled coquettishly, brushing a stray hair out of her eyes, and Peter was once again smitten by her beauty.

"Well, how can I resist, when you ask that way?" he said.

"There's one more thing," she said, smiling shyly. "Would you take your shirt off? I think it would give the photograph more character."

"Take my shirt off?" Peter said. "And give those animals more flesh to peck at? Are you daft, girl? Besides, what would your mother say? It's not the proper thing to do, is it?"

"Oh, don't bother about Mother," Victoria said. "She will never see this photograph, I promise you. It will be for my own personal use. I know it sounds bold, but I really would like you in profile against the sky, with your muscles exposed. Would you do it for me? Please?" She used that playful smile again, and once again he could not resist.

"I must be off my moorings, but I'll do it," Peter said, unbuttoning his shirt. "Just promise me this, my girl: That you'll take this blasted photograph quickly, before the mosquitoes make a dinner out of me."

"I promise!" Victoria said, laughing. "But you must hurry and get your shirt off."

Peter unbuttoned his shirt and draped it over a nearby rock, exposing his upper body to the sun. He felt naked in front of Victoria, and he was acutely conscious of her eyes on his skin.

Victoria directed him to stand next to the boat, looking out at the lake, with one foot on the upturned boat and "an attitude of expectancy", as she called it. The mosquitoes attacked him with vigor, and it was all he could do to keep from slapping at them.

"How much longer?" he pleaded, through gritted teeth. "I don't know if I can stand it another minute."

"Just a bit more," Victoria said. "I'm going as fast as I can."

There was so much to do to get the picture set up, and Victoria fussed around with the workings of the bulky camera, the angle and distance, the exact pose that Peter should adopt, all of it heightened by the electricity between them, especially when she touched his bare flesh to move him into the proper pose. Her skin smelled like lilac and musk, and her closeness was intoxicating.

Finally, though, the mosquitoes were too much. They swarmed on his body, and it felt like scores of tiny needles pricking his skin, raising red, itchy welts wherever they landed. Standing motionless in his pose was a difficult task, and his body glistened with sweat from the effort. After what seemed like an eternity Victoria finally took the picture, then several more just to make sure, till he was half-mad from the mosquito bites. The minute she said, "Done!" he turned and ran into the lake, diving headfirst when he got out to waist-deep water.

The bracing cold water was a shock at first, but it numbed the terrible itching and it got the nasty creatures off his hide. He dove under the water again, and came up laughing.

"I'm sorry, Miss Victoria," he shouted. "I just had to get them things off me. I'll be out in a minute."

He turned and swam further out in the lake, and reveled in the feel of the cool water against his skin. He had always enjoyed swimming in the lakes and streams of Ireland, and he had a powerful stroke, which carried him quickly out to deeper water.

He came up for air and turned to the shore just in time to hear a splash and see Victoria dive in.

He had a glimpse of white undergarments, and he quickly covered his eyes, then turned his back to the shore so as not to see Victoria in such an immodest state.

"Miss Victoria!" he shouted. "What are you doing?"

"It looked so appealing, I thought I would join you!" she said. She was still many yards away from him, splashing about in the water.

"But it's not proper what you're doing!"

"Why not?" she said, laughing. Her voice came across the water like the neighing of a horse.

"But you're a woman!" he sputtered. "And I'm your family's coachman! Good Lord, Miss Victoria, this is not a proper thing to do. Please get out of the water now. I promise I will not look."

Her laughter rang out across the water again. "I don't care what's proper, Peter. Those attitudes are so old-fashioned. If I want to take a swim in the lake, I'll take a swim! Propriety be damned!"

"Miss Victoria, please!" Peter said. "There's no need to talk like a drayman. Please get out of the water now. What will your mother say?"

"I don't care what my mother says," Victoria shouted. "I am a new woman, and I will do what I want! I will not sit at home and drink tea like my mother's generation. I want to be part of the world, to see its wonder and do adventurous things. Why don't you swim over here and join me? I'm not as good a swimmer as you, and I can't get out that far."

Peter kept his eyes firmly fixed on the horizon. "I will do no such thing, Miss Victoria. I am not so daft as that. I will not lose my position for a mad adventure like this. Have you lost your mind? Why, if your father found out --"

Just then there was the sound of splashing and turbulence in the water, from behind him. Victoria shouted, "Peter, help me! I have a cramp. I'm drowning!"

"You can't be drowning," Peter scoffed. "The water is not very deep where you are."

"I am too drowning!" she shouted. She was choking, as if she were swallowing water. "Help!" she shouted. "Peter, help me!"

Peter tried to stay calm. He did not want to turn around, but she sounded like she was in some distress. "Just put your feet on the bottom and walk out," he said. "I'm sure you can walk out to shore, Miss Victoria."

"No!" she shouted, coughing. "I cannot. I am in too deep. Help me!"

Peter felt trapped. This must be how people feel when they're going to their execution, he thought. There was nothing else to do, though, because she really did sound like she was drowning. He turned and swam back to her, his powerful arms slicing through the water. When he got to her she was flailing about in water that really was over her head, but Peter, because of his height, could stand up in. He put his arms around her and carried her like a baby to the shore. She was choking and coughing from swallowing water, and she rested her head on his shoulder, and clasped him about the neck. When he got to the beach he tried to set her down gently on the sand, but she held on to him fiercely and would not let go.

"Let me put you down, my girl," Peter said. "And we'll see what ails you."

Suddenly, Victoria stopped coughing, looked up at him through her wet lashes, stood up on her toes and kissed him full on the lips.

A shock ran through him, all the way to his toes.

And then he kissed her back.

CHAPTER FIFTEEN

In that moment Peter felt like a man on a high cliff who has just taken a leap into the empty air, and now he was heading straight for a pool of water far below. His shyness about looking at Victoria, his consciousness of their different stations in life, his fear of being dismissed from service -- all of it was gone as he fell headlong through the air.

He knew nothing except that she was a woman and he was a man, and everything started and ended with that.

He kissed her madly, recklessly, like a man possessed, and she responded in kind. Their lips were greedy, their tongues insistent. He had harbored a secret desire to touch her for so long, and now his fingers roamed over her body with ecstatic abandon. She was wearing a white linen chemise over a corset and white drawers, and the swell of her breasts felt like velvet to his fingertips. Somehow they ended up on the sand, with her on top of him, her mouth roaming his face and neck, planting kiss after kiss on them.

He was on fire with lust, and in no time he had her chemise off, and she had unhooked the top of her corset, releasing her breasts to the touch of his fingertips. She moaned with pleasure as he kissed her earlobe, and then rained kisses on her neck. Their bodies were covered with grainy sand now, and steam was coming off them. He cupped her firm buttocks and pulled her toward him, she held his head in her hands and kissed him fiercely.

It went on for how long he did not know, both of them swept along in a wave of passion that crested but never broke. They said things they would not remember; communicating in a language of moans and murmurs, the wordless language of the heart, the medium of delirious desire.

When the wave finally broke over them and receded they lay exhausted side by side, feeling the sun on their naked skin, smelling their musky sweat odor, and listening to the call of the loons on the lake and the gentle lapping of the water on the shore. The mosquitoes were gone, swept away by a breeze that pushed them off the water and into the forest.

Peter felt emptied of everything, in a sleepy haze that enveloped him like a warm blanket, and he floated along lazily, not wanting to wake up. He did not want to listen to that voice on the edge of his consciousness that was telling him he had done something terribly wrong.

In time, however, he heard splashing, and he raised his head to see Victoria swimming in water much farther out than where he had rescued her. She had a smooth, confident stroke, and he realized she had been in no danger when he had carried her to shore; she had planned the whole seduction.

There were times, and this was one of them, when Peter felt that his life was at the mercy of forces he could not control. As he sat and watched Victoria swimming back and forth, he suddenly felt like the world was closing in on him. It was not in his nature to worry, but at times like this the bottom dropped out of his confidence and he saw a black void yawning below.

"Why so glum, Mr. Morley?" Victoria said, as she came out of the water, her skin as smooth as a seal's and pink from the cold lake water. "You look as if someone just died."

"Sure and I'm thinking we should not have done what we did," Peter said.

"Why not? It was a wonderful, passionate thing to do," Victoria said, shaking the water out of her mane of blonde ringlets. "And it made me feel so good. Don't you feel good?"

"Of course," Peter said. "I feel tiptop, my girl. It's just that there are a few complications. For one, I'm your family's coachman. For another, I'm a married man, with two children."

"Oh, don't be such a bore, Peter," Victoria said, sitting down next to him. "This was just a pleasant diversion, a romp in the sun. It affects nothing, changes nothing. We will dry ourselves off, put our clothes on and go back to the house, and everything will be the same."

"The same?" Peter said. "How can everything be the same? Why, we have just done the marital act. We have shared the most intimate--"

Victoria threw her head back and laughed. She tried to speak several times, but each time she laughed harder, till her body was shaking and tears were running down her face.

"What in damnation is so funny?" Peter said.

Finally, Victoria got her composure back, and she said: "Really, Peter, you sound like a Presbyterian minister. It was a glorious, happy romp, but that is all. Now we must go back to our lives: I to my dinner parties and hobbies and gentleman callers, and you to your horses and your little Rose."

It was like a needle to his heart, so quick and sharp that it took his breath away. He was unable to speak for a moment. Finally, he managed: "Is that all it was to you?"

She laughed again, and now it sounded even more like the braying of a horse. "Of course, silly Peter! What else could it be?"

Things were different after that. Peter regained his hearty manner soon enough, and he told many humorous stories and jokes on the carriage ride back to the house. Underneath his happy exterior, though, he was aware of a grim fact: that Victoria and her kind would never see him as an equal. He was of the servant class, an ignorant mick to them, just one out of millions of poor, uneducated Irish that had come to this country in recent decades. He was there to serve them, to drive their horses and clean their houses and cook their meals, but never to presume to be their equal. Even an afternoon of passion on a beach was not enough for them to think of him as anything more than a useful accompaniment to their lives.

All of the good feelings, the wave of ecstasy he had felt, were now condensed in a little ball of anger inside him. It was like a stone in his stomach, a nasty hard thing that he could not digest. He could still smile, could still sing for them at their dinner parties and make them laugh with his jokes, but now he knew that the murderous, sick rage inside him would not go away.

He would not try to numb it with drink, the way so many of his countrymen had done. No, he would not let them put him in that box: "See, he's just another drunken Irishman." He had vowed back when he was Sean McCarthy not to take that route. He would be different, he would break out of the squalor he saw all around him, so much of it caused by people giving up, giving in to the defeat that had been their country's lot for hundreds of years.

It was a wounded Peter Morley who showed up at the door of their room in West Philadelphia at the end of that summer and took Rose in his arms. He was a man who needed the comfort of Rose, the balm of a woman who understood him.

But even so, the anger was still there.

It was there late at night, with the boys asleep as he and Rose made love under the sheets soaked with their sweat, while their Irish neighbors argued drunkenly or sang songs, and horses' hooves clop-clopped in the street outside. It was there when he walked in the park with his sons and saw the old Irish women pointing at them because they knew he had gotten Rose pregnant with Tim before they were married. It was there in the stink of horses that never left his clothing, the way he couldn't bring himself to go inside a church anymore, the way the shopkeepers would ignore him and lavish all their attention on Victoria or one of the other Lancasters if he went out with them.

He was nothing, a nobody. Invisible. It was the same here as in Ireland.

"You're a handsome man," Victoria's friends would say. "You have a voice fit for the stage." He knew he could sing and that he looked good.

He began to wonder if it was a way out, a path to a better life.

He could never be more than an amusing after dinner singer for the rich people, he knew that, but there were other places where he could try his luck at singing for an audience. There was no room for an Irishman on the stage, but there were saloons where the Irish went to drink away their sorrows, and they loved to hear songs that reminded them of their native land. Peter's high tenor voice would remind them of home, and they'd pay to hear him sing, he figured.

It would mean more time away from Rose, but it was a prospect that did not bother him. Indeed, his visits to her were full of arguments and shouting now, and the tears of his little boys, who did not understand why their father was so cross when he came home. His visit to Rose that late August night had produced a new baby boy, whom they named William, but instead of being proud and happy, it brought more gloom to Peter's heart.

One day when he was out with the boys he stopped in to a saloon called "Boyle's" in West Philadelphia. He told the saloonkeeper, a barrel-chested man with a thick mustache named Paddy Boyle, that he would sing on Saturday nights for whatever the customers would give him in tips.

Boyle wanted to hear him sing, so he broke into a version of "Dear Old Skibbereen" that had the big man sobbing by the last verse, and he slapped his hand on the bar and said, "Bedad, that's enough to make a man bawl his eyes out. You can start on Saturday night!"

"But we see you so little as it is," Rose said, when Peter told her of his new job. "Why must you rob us of what little time you have and give it to a bunch of rascals in a saloon?"

"Because I need more money to feed you and that gang of children," he said. "You don't want to starve, do you? I'm doing all I can for you, woman. Let me be."

He saw the sadness and the longing in Rose's eyes, but he put it out of his mind.

CHAPTER SIXTEEN

April 1895

Dearest Theresa,

I hope this letter finds you all in good health. It has been so long since I have received a letter from you, and I wish you would write to me more. I yearn to hear more about the family. Did you receive my last photograph? I wanted Father to see my darling boys, with the addition of little Willy now. They are growing up so well, and I do think that Willy looks like Father, don't you? His chin juts out like Father's when he is cross.

We are getting along in our lives. I have learned how to do knitting and lace making, and I make clothes for infants, little bonnets and christening dresses, which brings in some extra money for us. It is a blessing to be able to make a few extra dollars. The boys are growing, and we have had to rent rooms in a different section of the city because we needed a bigger place to live.

My husband Peter is doing well. He still works as a coachman for the Lancaster family, but now he makes some extra money by singing on Saturday nights at a saloon in town. It is not the type of place a woman would go to, so I have never seen him sing, but the men pay him well to sing songs that remind them of home. I am happy to have the extra money, because, as I said, we need it to live on.

Peter is a good man and is trying his best, but our situation is difficult. I hardly ever see him, because he is required to spend most of his time living with the Lancaster family. He is supposed to only get Thursday afternoons and Sundays off, but he has talked the family into letting him free on Saturday evenings so he can go to his singing engagement. When he gets home from the saloon it is usually early Sunday morning, and he is tired and sleeps most of the day on Sunday. We only have a few hours with him before he has to go back to the Lancasters. Most Thursday nights he sings as well, so we barely see him at all on those days. Little Tim says he hardly knows his father, and Paul acts shy with him. Baby Willy cries when Peter arrives, for he does not know this big man who picks him up from his cradle and sings to him.

It is a lonely life for me, and I often cry myself to sleep at night. I love my sons dearly, and I would not trade them for the world, but sometimes I feel I have come down mightily from my days working for the Lancasters. Then I lived in a fine great house and ate the best food and dressed in good clothes (not as pretty as Mary Driscoll did, but handsome clothing nevertheless), and I had a life filled with laughter, companionship and usefulness. Now I live in the humblest of rooms and I wear my dresses till they are frayed and worn, and I am always hungry from the meagerness of my diet. I worry always about money. There are times when I think I could go mad from worrying.

Please do not tell Father this, but last month the landlady threatened to turn us out because I owed her several months' rent. I begged her to let us stay, but I do not know how I will meet my rent payment this month.

I do have a bright spot in a certain priest who has been very kind to me. His name is Father Callan, and he is the rector of a church in the city. It is not a Catholic church, I am afraid. I have not felt welcome in my parish church for some time. One day last summer when I was at my wit's end I stumbled into an Episcopal church. Father Callan saw my state of nervous exhaustion and invited me and the children to supper. It was the kindest thing anyone had done for me in a long time, and I don't care if he is not a Catholic priest. Are you shocked by this? I know there is no love for Protestant clergy in our land, but this man has been a ray of sunshine to me. He buys some of my lacework for his altar, and has found me work making baby bonnets and christening dresses for his parishioners.

I try to go to Mass at his church, but it is far away and sometimes I cannot walk that far with the boys. Peter will not go to Mass with us. He has not been inside a church in many a year, but there is no talking to him about it. I worry for his eternal soul, but he gets red in the face whenever I bring the subject up.

Peter has his demons, I have learned, and they make his life difficult. There are times at night when he wakes up screaming from terrible nightmares, and it is all I can do to get him to stop. He usually wakes the boys with his outbursts, and then I have to get them all settled down before we can go back to sleep. Peter will not tell me what his dreams are about, but I think that something from his past is troubling him.

I have never met anyone like him. He says the past means nothing to him, and he is glad to be rid of it. He never speaks of any family back in Ireland, and says he has none. I tell him everyone has family and he must be connected to someone, but he brushes me off and will not discuss it. He is mad to make a new life for himself here, and talks of nothing but Progress and the wonders of this country, with all its inventions and gadgets and new ideas.

I do not understand a person who has no feeling for his family. I would feel cut off, lost and abandoned if I did not have family. I tell my boys about Skibbereen all the time. At night, before they go to bed, I sing them songs I learned as a girl, and I tell them about their aunts, Theresa and Annie, their Uncle Brian, and their grandfather Samuel. I tell them about the farm, nestled in a green valley, and the way the River Lee winds through the countryside on its way to the sea, and the place where you can stand on a hill and see the far off sea shining in the sun.

I hope and pray that I can bring my boys over some day so they can see their homeland.

That will not happen for many years, I am afraid, and I wonder if everything will be changed when we do come back. When you wrote to tell me Annie got married last Spring and moved to Liverpool, it was like a knife to my heart. I know that life is hard in Skibbereen and there is not enough work, so I do not blame her for moving away. It is the same thing I did, after all. But if everyone moves away, there will be no home left for us.

That is why I want to urge you not to drown in bitterness about your lot in life. I know it is hard staying at home and working on the farm, especially since Brian seems to do nothing but drink these days and Father is sick so much. You are needed there, dear Theresa. You are the glue that is keeping our family together. I am too far away, and I cannot even send money anymore. Besides, Father still wants nothing to do with me because of my shame. Brian is no help, and Annie moved away. It is up to you, Theresa, to keep the farm running and not let the creditors take it away. If I could trade places with you I would, although I could not bear to leave my sons.

Your lot is not easy, especially since there are so few men left to marry. It seems that our country is still suffering from the Famine, which started everyone going away on ships to find work in other countries. I see so many people here from Cork, and I often wonder who is left to work the farms? I hear stories about abandoned farms and empty houses and it makes me sad to think that our ancient land has fallen on such hard times. I pray the Land Reform movement succeeds, and the small farmers will be allowed to buy the land they have tilled for so many years. Maybe then Father will be able to buy his farm, and we will have a piece of earth to call our own.

You see I still say "we" and "our". I cannot help myself, I still feel a part of the family, even though I have not seen any of you for fifteen years. The past will never leave me. In fact, sometimes I think it haunts me.

There are many times on a hot summer afternoon when I sit on the iron fire stairs outside and think of home, and all the noise and the crowds on the street disappear and I am once again walking down the dirt road to Skibbereen with rain coming down in a cool mist on my face and the clouds parting to reveal a rainbow and the sound of horses whinnying in the fields next to the parson's house. Do you think me mad to say that? I sometimes wonder if my mind will become like dear Mother's, filled with fairies and strange visions, for there are times when I seem to see and hear things that are not there. Ah, but I have no time for that, I cannot go wandering about at night like she did, not when I have these three boys to look after. Pray for me, Theresa. You know that I pray for you all every night.

Your loving sister,

Rose

Rose folded the letter and put it in the envelope addressed to the Post Office in Skibbereen, then sealed it and put it aside. She was sitting at the kitchen table, writing by the light of a kerosene lamp. She turned the lamp down and went in the boys' bedroom to look at them. Tim was stretched out full length, taking up most of the bed he shared with Paul, who was curled up in a ball and looked ready to fall off the edge of his side. She went over and shifted them around so that Paul had more room. Little Willy was sucking his thumb peacefully in his wooden cradle next to their bed, and she marveled again at how he looked so much like her father.

It was so wonderful that God had done this, putting the stamp of her father on her baby's face. It soothed her loneliness to see the little face staring up at her, and made her think there was still a thread that tied her to the old homestead, even though so much had changed since she left.

These three boys were the biggest change. Fifteen years ago she had come here as a girl of eighteen, a country girl who knew nothing of the wider world. Now she was thirty three, a grown woman with a family. She had tasted the joys of intimacy with a man, only to find out that there were parts of him that he kept closed from her, and parts of her she could not open to him, which only made her loneliness more acute. She had worked in a grand house for a rich family, but now she was poor, counting her pennies and trying to hide from the landlady when she came calling for her money. She had seen marvels and wonders in this bustling, busy country, electric lights and music that came from machines, and streetcars, and even a contraption called an automobile that was supposed to be the next mechanical marvel. Instead of filling her with excitement, like it did Peter, it made her panic, because she could see the old life slipping away bit by bit with each new advance, each new marvel that came along. It made her feel like she was being carried away, like she was galloping down a dark country road on the back of a horse she could not control. She could feel herself losing her grip at times like this, when her head started pounding and her thoughts speeded up and came too close together.

"Do not worry, dear."

The voice was familiar, but it sent a shudder through her. She tiptoed out of the boys' bedroom, out to the kitchen where the voice had come from.

It was her mother, standing there in a halo of light from the kerosene lamp.

CHAPTER SEVENTEEN

Her mother was just as Rose remembered her: a shock of hair turned white prematurely, eyes that were twin pools of deepest blue, a black shawl wrapped around her, and a face that changed from dark to light and back again like the sea on a cloudy day.

"Get away from here," Rose hissed. Her knees were shaking, but she steeled herself to talk to this ghost. "You don't belong here. Off with you!"

Her mother smiled. "You don't recognize me, love of my heart?" She was talking in the Old Language, Gaelic, which Rose had never felt comfortable in, but somehow now she understood.

"Of course I recognize you," Rose said, and her heart swelled to see the image of her mother after so many years. Her throat closed up, and she could not speak for a minute. She sighed. "I don't know what you are, but saints preserve me, I am happy to see your face again." She gripped the back of a chair to hold herself steady, for she felt she could lose control at any moment. "It's been so long, and I missed you so much. You went away, and I never got to say goodbye."

"Sorry I am about that, dear Rose, but I had to go. 'Twas my time."

Rose wanted to embrace her, but she knew that would be foolish. This was not her mother, it was just a vision, as insubstantial as water. If she tried to go over and embrace this specter, she would be left clutching the empty air.

Her mother seemed so real, though, standing there. So much like the mother who had sown confusion, terror, and love in her memory.

And she was smiling. She seemed happy. It was the smile Rose remembered from early childhood, before her mother became consumed with the terrors that sent her out to wander alone across the fields and hills at night.

"Why are you here?" Rose said, folding her arms across her chest. She needed to know more before she could trust this vision.

"You have sons," her mother said. "May I see them?"

Rose remembered her mother's rantings about changelings. It was said in the old country that witches or fairies would come and steal a baby from its bed, and replace it with a fairy creature, a changeling that would look so much like the child it would fool everyone. Meanwhile, the real child was taken away to serve the creatures of the fairy world.

Rose was wary. "No," she said. "You cannot."

Her mother seemed unaffected. "No matter. I can come another time to see them. I will help you, Rose."

"What do you mean?"

"My Treasure, I come to tell you about the Good People," her mother said. Good People was what the old ones in Ireland called the fairies. You must always call them by that name, the old ones said, to avoid getting them angry.

"There are no Good People here," Rose said. "This is America. I have no use for that kind of talk. This is a different country, a different time."

"They are here too, Rose," her mother offered, smiling as if she were talking to a child who did not understand. "They are everywhere, and they are timeless."

"Wisha," Rose said. "Nonsense. I told you, I have no use for them."

"They can help you. They are good. They want only the best for us."

"Mother, I cannot listen to that. There are no Good People."

"They live in the forests and the glades," her mother said. "They come out at night and they dance. They dress in the most beautiful clothes, my darling, and they bow to each other like dukes and duchesses, and they dance all night long. Oh, the music they play! It is so beautiful to hear. They live in a timeless world, where there is no sadness, and no worry. Everything is always happy with them, Rose. I used to see them every night when I went out. Their world is so much brighter than ours."

The words were so seductive, and Rose felt them pulling her, pulling her toward the brightly lit world her mother had lived in. A world of spectral creatures and waking reveries, of visions full of splendid castles and grand ceremonies, of wishes fulfilled and dreams come true with the wave of a fairy hand.

And terrors that came in the night like the pooka, the midnight black horse that would carry people off to destruction in the sea.

"Stop your foolish talk," Rose hissed. "I cannot believe that rubbish. I live in this world, here," she said, sweeping her hand around the kitchen. "This is all that concerns me. I cannot believe in other worlds."

"And who would want to live in a world such as this?" her mother said. Sadness came into her eyes. "No my child, it is a place of pain and suffering, of hopes dashed and dreams broken. It is a cruel, heartless place you are in, Rose, and the sooner you learn that the better. Your life in this world is a hard thing, my daughter, and it will get harder. You will have more sadness. Your marriage is unraveling like an ill-made shawl, the seams coming apart. Your sons --"

But then she disappeared, fading away like the wisps of a dream at sunrise, or a snowflake in the palm of a hand. One moment she was there, the next she wasn't.

"My sons?" Rose said, clutching the chair. "What about my sons?"

It was too late. Her mother, or whatever it was that had appeared to her, was gone.

Rose sat down at the table and made the Sign of the Cross, then put her head in her hands. Was she losing her mind? Was she losing her grip and turning into a madwoman like her mother? That prospect had always frightened her, especially these last few years. There were times when she felt a loosening in her mind, a slipping, and she would hear the music of flutes, or strange voices at the very edge of her hearing. She would look around her on the street sometimes, to see who had called her name, and there was nobody but the busy, hurrying people walking by, their faces blurring into one blank anonymous face, and she knew no one was paying her any mind.

It was true her life was hard, that her heart yearned for tenderness and a warm embrace, but she could not start believing in fairies. That would not make anything better, would it?

It was disturbing, that she had seen her mother in a vision. What was it the ghost had started to say about her sons? She got up trembling and went back in the room to look at them. They slept peacefully, their beautiful faces rapt, "dreaming of Heaven" as the old people used to say. If anything happened to them she could not bear it. She would rather rip her beating heart from her breast than that anything bad should happen to these beautiful boys.

She closed their door and went back to the kitchen, taking the chipped blue teapot from the stove and pouring herself a cup of tea. She had to admit the vision of her mother was probably right about her marriage. For a while now Rose had known things were coming apart, and she was at a loss to know how to put them back together.

Just then there was the sound of footsteps on the stairway and then a knock at the door. It was Peter, fresh from his Thursday night of singing at the saloon. She knew he would be brimming with energy, unable to sit down, and yet surly and sarcastic, as he was most times now when she saw him. He was not happy to be around Rose and the boys, and he could not hide it.

Should she tell him about her vision? Should she tell him what her mother said about her marriage unraveling? What good would that do? It would just give him more reason to feel cut off from her. He did not believe in visions and fairies. They were part of a past he did not wish to know about, a past he wanted to be free of. To tell him what she saw and heard would only drive him away sooner.

And she knew he was halfway gone as it was.

CHAPTER EIGHTEEN

June 1897

The summers were blissful times for Peter. It was not just that he got to leave his problems with Rose behind when he went to Maine with the Lancasters. It was that he got to spend more time with Victoria.

He knew that Victoria did not love him, and he knew that he did not love her. It was nothing to cry about, was it? He would never be an equal in her eyes, and there was no changing that. He was a dreamer, it was true, but he knew when to shut off his dreams.

To be sure, he was not the type of man who would fall madly in love with a woman who did not love him back. He would not leave his heart so unprotected, so naked, as that.

Even so, being with her gave him a sense of possibility, of the richness of what Life had to offer. She had grown into a woman who wanted to live her life to the fullest, and she took delight in upsetting conventional ways of thinking.

"It's a bold new world out there, Peter," she would say. "We must take advantage of it."

She had read a story in the newspaper about a new vehicle made in Springfield, Massachusetts, called a Duryea Motor Wagon. The year before, in 1895, this contraption had won a race in Chicago against other motorized carriages. This summer on the way to Maine she made her father and Peter get off the train in Springfield so that she could see one of these new machines.

She was not disappointed. Frank Duryea, one of the inventors, gave Victoria, her father, and Peter a ride in the vehicle, which was exactly like a small carriage without a horse, and with a noisy, smelly engine in the rear. It puttered along at the speed of 7 miles an hour, a fact that Frank Duryea yelled proudly above the noise of the engine.

"Isn't this glorious?" Victoria shouted, sitting between Peter and Frank Duryea, her blonde hair blowing in the wind and her eyes aglow with excitement.

Peter shared her enthusiasm, marveling at the way the carriage moved under its own power.

"You're looking at the future, Peter," she shouted, elbowing him in the ribs for emphasis. "There won't be any need for coachmen in twenty years."

Back on the train to Maine, Victoria raved about the horseless carriage. "This machine will change everything, Father," she said. "You'd better get out of the train business. Nobody will want to ride these dirty old things anymore when they can have the thrill of riding in a motor car. Think of it! You could go anywhere you want, anytime you want. It's a miracle!"

Her father smiled indulgently and said, "I'm not convinced, my dear. It could very well be just a novelty. A fad. People may be interested in it for a few years, but then it will fade from view. I suspect no one will want to put up with the noise and unreliability of those contraptions. And look how fast we're traveling!" he said, tapping his hand against the windowpane as the landscape went rushing by. "Why, I don't see how those carriages could ever attain the speed of a good, well-built locomotive. Still, it bears watching. The rate at which new inventions become part of our lives these days is amazing. I grew up in a time of candlelight and horse-drawn wagons, and now we have electric lights and railroads. The world of my youth is gone forever."

The next day, as Victoria and Peter lay next to each other on their beach after a session of lovemaking, she turned to him and said, "What did you think of the Duryea motor carriage? You never said."

"I think it's a marvel, to be sure," Peter said. "And I expect you're right, it will do away with the likes of me. If ever they make those things cheap enough for the average man to buy, everyone will have one. You can put all the horses out to pasture, and turn the coachmen out, for there'll be no more traveling by horse."

"Aren't you glad you work for a progressive family like us?" Victoria said. "You saw the handwriting on the wall, as it were. Most coachmen probably don't realize they're in a dying field."

She was right. It was exciting to be around the Lancasters, much more exciting than to be at home with his Rose and their three sons. When he went home all Rose wanted to talk about was her lack of money, the trouble that Tim was getting into in school, and how she missed her family back in Ireland.

Even the singing he did was not bringing him any more pleasure, since he had to sing those maudlin Irish songs for the workingmen crowded into the saloons, and pretend to be an Irish patriot when he would not have gone back for all the money they could stuff into his pockets.

He wanted something different. He had big dreams, and he wanted to see them come true. Being around Victoria made him feel alive, full of the excitement of new things, new adventures, new sensations.

The first week in Maine that summer she unpacked one of the new Edison recording machines, something she had bought in Philadelphia. "Now you'll hear what a wonderful voice you have," she said. "Because we can record you on this machine."

It was a complicated, heavy metal thing and Peter did not understand the workings of it, but she had him sing a song into the bell of it and then it whirred and went to work, and later she was able to play it back. He was astonished to hear the tinny sound of his own voice coming out of that box. He filled up with tears and his heart pounded in his chest. To think that high, sweet voice was his! He had never dreamed it sounded quite like that, and it astounded him.

All that summer Victoria played the wax cylinder with Peter's song on it, and everyone who heard it clapped and cheered for it. Peter blushed with pride, and marveled each time that his voice could come out of a machine like that.

It excited him, made his blood rush, and made him want Victoria even more. She represented the new, the bold, the engine of possibility, and he wanted to claim it for his own.

Once, when nobody was home in the house, Victoria played the cylinder again, and a wave of passion came over them, so that they made love right on the couch in the parlor, with the breeze flapping the drapes and the sun beating down through the windows. Victoria screamed and Peter gasped, and they writhed like drowning people as the torrent of passion picked them up and took them far, far away from themselves.

At times like this Peter almost forgot he had a family. Rose wrote him letters, many letters, and he dreaded opening them to read her endless catalogue of sorrows, the list of troubles that burdened her and weighed him down with guilt.

He could not bring himself to write back. He was not much of a writer, and when he did sit down he was overwhelmed by the effort of trying to write something pleasant to her. So many thoughts went through his mind, but he did not know how to express them to her. How could he tell her that he was intoxicated by the newness all around him, that the thought of how the world was changing every day here in America almost drove him mad with glee? He could not fathom how she did not appreciate this. All she talked of bored him. He knew he should feel close to her and the boys, but his heart had no pull towards them.

Especially the oldest boy, Tim. Peter had never felt especially close to that one. There was always the specter of Martin Lancaster in the background whenever he thought of Tim. The boy did not especially look like Martin, but he did not look like Peter either. He had Rose's wounded look about him, and a soft mouth that seemed made for crying.

And he did cry, too. He cried or was angry most of the time. Perhaps it was because he knew his father did not love him.

Peter was feeling trapped, there was no other word for it. He had never wanted this, never wanted to be responsible for anyone, and now he had four people dependent on him. He sent money to Rose, but it was never enough. Her letters came every week, with more requests for money. "The boys need new shoes," or, "I have the rent due next week; please send something". He was not able to make any extra money by singing in the summer, for there were no saloons in the woods of Maine where he could find work.

He looked forward to his afternoons on the beach with Victoria. It was a time when he could forget all his cares and simply enjoy the pleasures of her body and the feel of sun and lake water on his skin.

One day she broke the spell. They were eating a picnic lunch under a tree after their hour of lovemaking, and she had packed fried chicken, some apples, grapes, and walnuts, and a bottle of cold, clear white wine. Victoria had a blanket wrapped around her and Peter sat in his white cotton drawers, enjoying the feel of the sun on his shoulders.

"And how is your little family?" Victoria asked, sipping from her wine glass. "Do you miss them?"

"No," he said, surprising himself with such an honest answer. "I do not miss them, not when I am here with you."

"You surprise me," she said.

"Do I? I should never have gotten married in the first place. It was only your father and mother who made me do it. Rose is a good girl, and we had some grand times together, but I was never in love with her."

"You have three children, do you not?"

"Aye, three boys. A man would be proud and happy to have three fine boys like them. I am ashamed to say that I don't feel that way. No, I don't feel close to the lads. It takes a lot of money to support a family like that, and I am always short of it. I sometimes wonder how I got myself in this predicament. God forgive me, but often it is that I think of leaving Rose and the boys."

"I understand the Catholic faith does not permit you to divorce," Victoria said, sipping her wine again.

"Aye, I am not the most churchgoing of men, Victoria," Peter said, "but I was raised in that faith and I cannot go against it. I would sooner cut off my arm than divorce Rose. No good Catholic Irishman or woman in the whole city of Philadelphia would have anything to do with me if I committed a sin like that.

"I don't know what to do, sometimes," he added, shaking his head. "Did you ever feel like you were trapped?"

"Always," she said. "I am trapped by the expectations my family has for me. Trapped by the life that is waiting for a woman of my class. I will not accept it, though! You can always break free, especially now. The world is heading toward a new century. Imagine! We are on the cusp of the 20th century. There is a sense of promise in the air. So many new things to be excited about, Peter! We must break out of the old molds, and embrace the new."

"They're lovely words you're speaking," Peter said. "Sure, and I'd like to believe them." He looked down at the ground and saw a column of ants marching toward the blanket Victoria had spread for their picnic. He scooped up a handful of dirt with the lead ant on it, and watched as it kept marching across the palm of his hand. "But look at this little fellow," he said. "He probably thinks the world is full of promise, too, my girl. Why, there's a nice big chicken leg in sight, and he's on his way with his friends to get some pieces of it and bring them back to their colony. He's thinking the world is a pretty good place, wouldn't you say?" Then he closed his fingers and squashed the ant, and wiped it off on a blade of grass.

"But then something comes along and changes it all," Peter continued. "Something he cannot control. Isn't that the way of all life? We're all just ants, Victoria, dreaming that we have control over our lives, when at bottom we're at the mercy of forces we can't see."

Victoria laughed, throwing her head back in the way that Peter found so attractive. "I didn't know you were such a philosopher, Peter. My goodness, but you think deeply about these things."

"Don't you agree, though? Aren't we all just like these fellows?" Peter took his shoe and brought it down hard on the column of ants, killing dozens of them and scattering the rest.

"No, I don't think so," she said. "We may not understand all of the forces at work around us, but we will in time. And we can always do our best to change them. I am optimistic, Peter. I will not be forced into a life of domestic servitude, like my mother and her generation. I believe I can lead a different life than her. I will not marry the man my parents choose for me, and I will have a career, and I will continue to work on the things I am passionate about, like women's suffrage. There are so many possibilities out there, and I am determined to make the most of them."

"Ah, girl, it makes me excited just talking to you," Peter said. "Come here and let me feel you next to me. Why, I can believe anything with you in my arms."

He reached over and kissed her, and immediately she cast the blanket aside and wrapped her arms around him. Her skin was warm and soft, and her breasts pressed against him insistently. He ran his fingers along her neck and she quivered with anticipation. Then they were on the blanket, scattering the plates and cups and food in the heat of their passion.

She moaned softly as he ran his tongue along her neck and down to the hollow between her neck and shoulder. Her body shivered and she pulled him to her with surprising force. Then she was directing him, guiding him along the currents of her body, taking him far out on the great swells of passion that swept across her seas. They were like shipwrecked sailors, clinging for life to each other, in a great fathomless sea of primal lust. Time ceased, and the sun stopped its circuit in the sky. They were conscious of nothing save the feel of skin on skin, the soul's cry of longing, and the need for union. They urged each other on with words, meaningless words, sounds that had no currency except in the heart's secret language.

Higher and higher they went, twisting and writhing, now fighting the current, now riding with it, finally guiding each other over the crest, exploding in profound joy, and then the long sweet drawback of the wave that left them gasping and drained of everything, sodden with release.

They had many afternoons like that all summer, and although Peter marveled at what heights they reached, the intense closeness that he had felt with no other woman, he knew deep inside that nothing would ever come of it. For all her talk of freedom and overcoming old barriers, all her slogans and crusades and scrambling after new things, Peter knew there was a line he could never cross. He was Peter the Irish coachman to her, and that alone would mean she could never fall in love with him. There was no mixing of the classes in America, just as there had not been in Ireland.

And yet, there was still the case of Martin Lancaster. He was a railroad executive now, just like his father, and he was busy at his job in Philadelphia most of the summer. He came up to Maine for only brief visits, but each time he would ask Peter, with feeling in his eyes, how Rose was doing. He did not seem to be interested in young women of his social station, much to the distress of his mother, who was always trying to make a match for him with the daughter of one friend or other.

Every time Martin asked about Rose, Peter would watch him carefully, trying to read his heart from the expression on his face. He never lost the suspicion that Martin and Rose had been lovers and Tim was their child. Rose rarely spoke of Martin, but the tenderness with which Martin asked about her made Peter wonder if he had been forced to marry Rose simply to give a name to another man's child. It left him feeling angry that he was trapped in a situation like this all to provide cover for Martin and Rose.

He often thought of asking Victoria about it, to see if she could offer information that would ease his mind. One day at the beach, they were sitting together by the overturned boat, and Peter said: "It seems odd that your brother has not found a woman to settle down with."

"Martin?" she said, as if the thought of his bachelorhood had never crossed her mind. "I know Mother fusses about that. He's 30 years old, and she thinks he should have found a wife by now. I guess he has not met the right girl, though. Why do you ask?"

"I don't know," Peter said. "I just thought a fine gentleman like him would have his pick of the lasses. He's a handsome man, well-spoken, from a good family, with plenty of money. He has all the advantages, I'd say."

"I suppose he's not interested in any of the girls he's met," Victoria said, stretching her body and yawning like a cat in the sun. "Nobody has turned his head like your Rose, I guess."

It was like being doused with icewater, and Peter reeled. "My Rose?" he said, raising his eyebrows. "What on Earth do you mean?"

Victoria laughed. "Surely you must have noticed how he got all goggle eyed around her. I used to tease him about it. He was like a teenage boy, for goodness' sake! Whenever he saw Rose he went weak in the knees."

"You don't say?" Peter said. "I never noticed."

"Well, it was obvious to me," she said. "I was almost ready to tell Mother about it. She and Father had no idea. I did not want to see Rose dismissed from our house, however. I admit I had selfish reasons -- she was my favorite of all the servants we ever had. Aside from you, of course," she said, blinking her lashes coquettishly. "I knew that Mother would get rid of Rose if she had the slightest inkling of Martin's feelings for her. She would not stand for it -- her adored son, falling in love with an Irish servant? It would be an embarrassment, and she would have hacked it off at the roots. Rose would have been dismissed on the spot. Luckily for us, you solved the problem, dear Peter, when you got Rose in a family way and had to marry her. She was removed from the household, and all of Martin's troubles vanished."

Peter flinched at the cold, heartless way she summed up the situation.

Once again he realized how high the wall was between him and the Lancasters. It would never be surmountable, not by him or Rose -- or even Martin, it seemed.

CHAPTER NINETEEN

December 24 1899

"What was he doing this time, Officer?" Rose said to the large policeman standing at her door with her son Tim in tow. She knew Officer Dooley well, since he had often brought Tim up the three flights of stairs to her apartment after catching him in some mischief.

"I caught the scamp stealing oranges from Mrs. Brennan's market again," Officer Dooley said. "They're the new California oranges, shipped here on the railroad, and Mrs. Brennan is very proud of them. Your boy was putting them in his pockets and was about to run away when I collared him. I keep a watchful eye on young Master Tim, and he'll not be getting away with any of his pranks when I'm on duty."

Tim would not look at Rose, but his arms were crossed and his chin stuck out defiantly, and Rose knew he would never admit his guilt.

"Did he damage anything?" Rose said.

"No damage this time," the policeman said. "I got him before he could throw the oranges at the passengers of a passing streetcar, like he did the last time. He certainly made a mess of that fine lady's dress, and I didn't want something like that to happen again."

Rose sighed. These visits from the police were becoming a more common affair, as Tim seemed to be finding more ways to cause mischief than ever before. He could be such a sweet boy at times, when he would put his head in his mother's lap and listen quietly as she told a story to him, but at other times the hurt inside would get the better of him, and all he wanted then was to lash out, to hurt someone else as a way of making his own pain go away.

"I thank you, Officer Dooley," Rose said. "I appreciate all you've done for us."

"It's no trouble," the policeman said. "I feel sorry for the lad, knowing the facts about him as I do."

Rose saw the hurt flash in Tim's eyes once more. The policeman was referring to the fact that Tim was born out of wedlock, a fact that seemed eternally present to the Irish in West Philadelphia. The neighborhood was like a village back in Ireland, the way everyone knew everyone else's business, and they were not shy about bringing it up again and again.

"Thank you for your concern," Rose said. She took Tim by the shoulder and brought him inside. "I'll handle this now. Have a good day, Officer."

"Good day, ma'am," Officer Dooley said, touching his fingers to his hat. He turned to Tim and wagged his finger, saying, "You mind your mother, you little pagan. I know you don't go to church, but that's still no excuse for getting in to so much mischief. God sees you whether you're in church or out." He turned, strode to the stairwell and went down the stairs, his boots clicking on each step, and Rose closed the door.

Inside, she tried once again to be firm.

"Sit down, young man," she said, and Tim took a seat at the kitchen table, his chin sticking out and his hands clenched into fists.

"How many times do I have to find Officer Dooley at my door, telling me again about your pranks? Have you no shame, Timothy Morley? Why do you do these things?"

"Where is my father?" Tim said. "Why doesn't he visit us?"

Rose sighed once again.

"I told you before, son, he has to work today. We will see him tomorrow afternoon."

"But it's Christmas Eve," Tim said, his lower lip jutting out defiantly. "He should be with us on Christmas Eve."

"He has to work at the Lancasters. They need him there tonight, because they have a tradition of visiting their friends on Christmas Eve, and he has to drive them around. Now, why don't you be a good boy and play with your brothers? Paul and Willy are out at the playground. I'm sure they're having lots of fun, and you could join them. I need to finish making a christening dress this afternoon. After that I'll make a nice supper. I bought a bit of ham from Mrs. Brennan, and we'll have some boiled potatoes. It will be a grand Christmas Eve dinner."

"I don't like ham," Tim said. "And I'm sick of potatoes. I wish we could eat a Christmas goose, like other people."

"We don't have the money," Rose said, hating herself for uttering that phrase so often. "I'm sorry, Tim, but a fat goose costs more money than I have in my purse."

"Money!" Tim snapped. "It's always about money. Why doesn't my father give us more money?"

"He gives us all he can," Rose said. "And lucky we are that he has a job in the first place. The times are hard, my son, and there is the devil of a lot of people out of work. We should thank God your father gives us what he is able to. Now go outside like a good boy and play with your brothers. And no more getting into trouble!"

She leaned over and tried to kiss him, but he bolted out of his chair and ran out the door, and she could hear his footsteps all the way down the three flights of stairs, then the door slamming as he went out.

She went over to the kitchen table and put her head in her hands. She should be working on that christening dress, because the sooner she finished it the sooner she'd get paid, and she needed money more than ever this Christmas. She had no gifts for the boys, and a scrawny tree with a few handmade decorations on it in the corner of the kitchen was the only sign of Christmas in the room. She would have liked to buy a goose to cook so she could give her sons a proper Christmas, but once again she felt like she was shortchanging them, not giving them the kind of childhood they would remember with happiness, the way she remembered her own childhood in Skibbereen.

The sadness hit her like a wave, and instead of holding it back the way she did so many times, she let it wash over her. She let the tears come, till they were streaming down her face. She wept until her body shook, letting all the sadness out. It was so hard to have her life turn out like this. She was only 35, but sometimes she felt like an old woman. She hardly ever smiled anymore, and she lay awake at night and tried to come to grips with the fact that her husband did not love her, and did not even seem to care for the three boys he'd had with her.

In the background, always, she heard those whispers on the edge of her consciousness, whispers that she tried hard to ignore. She had had no more visits from the ghost of her mother, but sometimes it seemed all she had to do was let her guard down and there her mother would be, smiling and talking to her.

There was a knock at the door, and Rose quickly dried her tears. She assumed it was Officer Dooley bringing Tim back for pulling another prank, or perhaps that cranky old Mrs. Noonan who lived downstairs had caught the boy teasing her dog again. It wouldn't do to have anyone see her crying; she especially did not want Tim to see her showing such weakness.

She opened the door, and there in the doorway, was Martin Lancaster.

He stood there in a black overcoat and a stylish pearl gray Homburg hat, which he took off quickly. He was carrying packages wrapped in brown paper and tied with ribbons.

"Hello, Rose," he said. "May I come in?"

Rose was speechless. Finally, she blurted out, "Martin? Is it you? What are you doing here?"

Martin smiled. "I know it's been a long time, Rose, but I always thought of you. I used to ask Peter about you, but after a while he seemed to be annoyed with my questions, and I gathered things were not going well. He spends a lot of his free time at our house, and does not seem to come home to you very much. I know you have three children, and, well, I guess I was just concerned about you. I have some Christmas gifts here," he held the packages up.

There was an awkward silence as Rose simply stared at him.

Then, he cleared his throat and said once again, "May I come in?"

Rose stood aside and let him walk by her, as stunned as if she were being visited by a ghost. She had not seen Martin Lancaster in ten years. In that time he had changed from a boy into a man, from a college student to a man in his early thirties, with the imprint of success on him, the solidity of a man who has earned a spot in the world. His sandy hair was thinning on top, but his face had filled out to a pleasing squareness that combined well with his sensitive lips and warm brown eyes.

"May I sit down?" he said, and Rose finally came out of her reverie.

"Of course," she said. "Let me take your coat. Would you like some tea? I am sorry, but I cannot offer you more than that. I have not been to the grocer's yet today, and there is little I have here in the way of food."

"Tea would be nice," Martin said, taking off his overcoat and giving it to her. He sat at the kitchen table and watched as she fussed about with the teapot, pouring two cups and bringing out the chipped sugar bowl, all the time talking rapidly.

"How are things at home?" Rose chattered. "I imagine little Tom must be all grown by now. Oh, how I remember what a bright-eyed young boy he was! Peter keeps me informed, of course, but he forgets to tell me some things. I wonder has Victoria met a nice young man yet? I am sure your mother would like her to do so. And your father's health, how is that? I always admired him so mumch. It was a pleasure to work for such a fine family as yours. . ."

"Rose, I have missed you so much," Martin said, suddenly.

Rose poured his tea with a trembling hand, and when she spilled some of it, he put his hand over hers. "Sit down, Rose," he said.

She sat down, her heart beating so loud she was afraid he would hear it.

"I came here because I wanted to bring your boys some Christmas presents," he continued. "But that was just an excuse. I wanted to see you again, Rose. I have lived in agony since you left our home. I have tried to forget you for ten years, but I cannot. I am in love with you, Rose."

Rose dropped her teacup on the linoleum floor, where it shattered into jagged shards.

"Oh, no," she said, reaching down to pick up the pieces. "I only have four of these cups, and now one of them's gone."

"Please," Martin said, grabbing her wrist. "Let me do that." He looked at her, his face close to hers, and then before she knew what was happening, she was in his arms, and they were kissing passionately. Her blood was in her face, and her heart pounded in her ears like the hooves of a racehorse. Rose kissed him hungrily, like a starving person who has stumbled into a wedding feast before the guests have arrived, and is trying to fill her need with one eye on the door.

His arms were a shelter, a warm place offering protection from the storm, and Rose sank into them with gratitude. She had never kissed Martin Lancaster before, although she'd often imagined what it would be like. He was so tender and loving now, and she could not pull herself away from him.

They ended up on the ancient blue sofa, their bodies entwined and their lips meeting each other in passionate tumult.

Martin ran his hands through her hair, loosening the places where it was tied up, and murmured about how beautiful it was. He kissed her neck tenderly, and the hollow between her neck and shoulder, and it made her shiver with excitement.

She knew it was wrong, so wrong. She was a married woman, her boys could come bursting in the door at any moment, and besides, he was a Lancaster, a member of a different class. People weren't supposed to act this way.

But her need was so great. Peter had shut her out long ago, and she had such an aching black hole inside, a place where the sadness never went away. She could not stand the loneliness anymore, her body responded almost against her will to Martin's gentle touch, and she kissed him greedily, throwing caution to the wind.

Finally, with great effort, she tore herself away from him, and moved to the other side of the couch. She was panting as if she had run a long distance, her face was flushed, and her hair was falling down in strands across her eyes.

"We cannot do this," she managed to say. "My sons are playing outside. They could come in."

"I understand," Martin said. "I have no wish to disrupt your life, Rose. I only wanted to see you again, after so long. It has been difficult, so difficult, to live without you." He was red in the face also, and breathing heavily. His kind, sensitive brown eyes looked wounded with the agony of unrequited love. "I am so sorry," he said. "I did not mean for this to happen."

He stood up. "I will go now. I won't bother you again."

"No," Rose said, standing also. She leaned up and kissed him, then put her head on his neck. Tears were starting to fill her eyes. "I cannot bear that. I need to see you again, Martin. Please."

CHAPTER TWENTY

Peter watched the motor car coming down Broad street, its driver clad in a long dun-colored coat, gloves, goggles, cap, and a red scarf that was flying jauntily in the breeze. The man was honking his horn furiously as he made his way through the carriages, streetcars, and pedestrians. The engine made an infernal clanking noise, and spooked some of the horses, leaving many people shaking their fists at the car in exasperation, but as it passed in front of City Hall where Peter was standing, he once again felt like he was looking at the future. He had heard of these types of machines before: they were called "wagonettes" and they were made by the Keystone Company, a local firm that designed and manufactured its own motor cars. A friend of Mr. Lancaster's was one of the principal investors.

Peter waved to the driver as he passed, and clapped his hands in admiration.

Once a novelty, these machines were now slowly becoming more commonplace. Peter had seen half a dozen of them driving the streets of Philadelphia in the last two months. As the days got closer to the new year and the new century, Peter felt sure that these contraptions would make a bold change in people's lives.

Many people disagreed, feeling that the machines were at best a nuisance and at worst a hazard, causing horses to stampede, carriages to overturn and their passengers to be injured.

Not Peter. He was itching to drive one. The ease of movement, the fact that you could just get in the vehicle, start it up, and it would take you anywhere, was intoxicating. That was true freedom, he thought. Why, you could get in one and drive away from your old life, just leave all the ugliness and tragedy behind, and start fresh.

He wanted badly to start fresh. There was a new century coming, and the air was filled with the smell of promise, like the air after a spring shower. The world was poised for new growth, just like in spring, and Peter wanted to be a part of it. He wanted to bloom anew, to grow, to be something different.

Always when he got caught up in ecstasies of thought like this, though, he had to come back to Earth. There was his past in

Ireland, the face of the man he killed that never left him, and of course, over here there were Rose and his children.

That is why he was here, walking up to the big brass doors of Wanamaker's Grand Depot, the emporium where you could find just about anything to buy. It was Christmas Eve and Peter was here to buy presents for Rose and the boys.

He did not know where to start. The last year had been a bad one for their marriage. The distance between him and Rose seemed to be growing farther by the day. He had avoided going home to her for long stretches, and he found the prospect of seeing her and the boys daunting. She had taken to writing him letters not just when he was in Maine, but when he was living with the Lancasters just 20 miles away from her in Chestnut Hill, and the letters were filled with longing, sadness, complaints. There was never enough money, time, or love that he could give them. She needed too much, and he was conscious of his lack, of the hole inside him that could never supply her and the boys with what they truly wanted.

He avoided church, but that didn't change the fact that he knew he was a sinner. The burden of his sins was harder and harder to bear. He had killed a man, which was bad enough. Added to that, though, he had committed adultery with Victoria. And him a married man with three sons!

He tried to put it out of his mind, although he knew he could not do so for very long. He understood why so many of his countrymen took to drink to forget their troubles. He had been tempted many times himself, but he had seen too much of the destruction that whiskey caused among the Irish, and he had never wanted to go down that road.

He went up the grand marble staircase of Wanamaker's store and followed the signs to the toy section. He had the next twenty-four hours off and he needed to buy some presents and try to make amends, to make a good Christmas for his wife and sons. He found the toy department and began to look at the selection of shiny new toys. He would buy something merry for the boys; that would make them happy. He looked at the metal soldiers, tops, hoops, and marbles, thinking how much luckier these boys were than he had been in his own childhood. He had played with no toys as a boy. There were no luxuries like that in his blighted, godforsaken childhood. He had worked always, as far back as he could remember, doing any kind of work for a shilling or two. He'd learned early that he could sing a tune well, and he earned a few coins with his voice, singing at fairs and dances and country festivals, but it was never enough. He'd always had to find other work, usually of the lowest kind, like mucking out the stables for the British soldiers, or cleaning their latrines.

He picked up a cast iron metal soldier, hand-painted and weighty, wearing the field uniform of a British soldier, complete with a tiny service carbine at the ready. It reminded him of the crisp uniforms of the British soldiers he'd seen at home, and the thought brought the sharp pain of remembrance, the vision of the lieutenant lying bloody on the floor, dead, and the stark terror that had driven him to leave Ireland forever.

"Oh, dear, is that the last one?" came a voice from behind him.

He turned to see a petite woman in a pearl gray suit standing next to him looking at the soldiers. She had sandy blonde hair tied up like a Gibson Girl, and she had fair skin and merry gray-green eyes. She was carrying several packages, wrapped with colorful ribbons, and it was obvious she had been Christmas shopping.

"Yes, I think it is," Peter said, noticing there were no more like it in the display of soldiers.

"Were you going to purchase it?" the woman said. She had a mild British accent, Peter noticed. "You look like you're ready to buy it. It's just, well, if you are not thinking of buying it I would certainly like to. I have only one more present to get, and I have a nephew who would adore that."

"Oh, to be sure, you can have it," Peter said, handing it to her with a flourish.

"Are you certain?" she said. "I don't mean to be rude. I don't want to take it and deprive your son."

She had perfect white teeth and a tight little smile that gave off a conspiratorial air, as if she was sharing a private joke with him. Peter was captivated by her.

Somehow he did not want her to know that he had a son. "It's for my, ah, nephew," he said. "And you can have it, ma'am."

"I'm not usually this forward," she said. "Are you sure? Don't you like it?"

"Why, it's a nice enough toy, I suppose," Peter said. "If I'm going to buy a toy soldier, though, I'd be more wanting to buy an American one. One of those blue coated men who won the West."

"I see," the woman said. "Then you're not British? Something about you made me think you were."

Peter smiled. "Do I still look like I'm from over there? I've been in America for twenty years, more or less, and I thought I was quite the Yankee. I suppose not. Actually, it's Ireland I'm from, but then, that's under the King's dominion, isn't it?"

"Why yes," she said. "Though some of the Irish don't seem to think so. But, no matter, the point is, you're not from this place, are you? It's the same with me. No matter how long you live in this country, it will never be home, I fear. I have been here two years, but I have not adapted. I miss England dearly, and I cannot wait to go back." She smiled again, and once more it was as if she were sharing something with him alone.

"I only came here to help my brother when his wife got sick," she continued, "and I look forward to the day when I can sail back to my dear homeland. But, listen to me, prattling on like this. As if you'd want to stand here on Christmas Eve and listen to the boring details of my life! I will let you get back to your shopping. Good day, sir."

But Peter did not want her to go. "May I help you with those packages?" he said. "You look burdened."

"Are you quite sure?" the woman said. "Although, I would not mind some help, come to think of it. I am afraid I bought too many presents, but I wanted to make a memorable Christmas for my brother and his family. I am just now going to catch a train to New Jersey. The family is expecting me back for Christmas Eve dinner."

"Then I am happy to walk you to the train station," Peter said, smiling. He took some of her packages and escorted her down the grand staircase and out to the street, where the sky had turned pearl gray and a steady fall of snow had begun.

"Now look at that!" the woman said. "Isn't it perfect? I do so much love to see snow on Christmas. We never got much of it in the little town where I grew up, but once when I was a girl it snowed on Christmas Eve, and it made me so happy."

"I know what you mean," Peter said, as they made their way down the crowded street toward the train station. "It makes everything seem bright and gay. Adds a bit of excitement, too, don't you think? Why, a snowfall makes the world seem fresh and new, the way it covers everything in a blanket of white, and every step you take is a new path through it."

"That's a lovely way to put it." She gave him that smile again. There was a shyness about it, an English reserve, which made it even more special when she shared it with you. She had a pert little English nose and those gray-green eyes, and dimples. She was much smaller than Peter, barely coming up to his shoulder, but her petite body seemed perfectly proportioned. Peter felt his spirits lift around her, and there was a buoyancy that almost made him feel like he was floating on air.

They made their way along Market Street, part of a happy crowd of people heading home for Christmas Eve. People were carrying their beribboned packages, everyone flushed with excitement and laughing at the magical fall of snow on Christmas Eve. A group of children was singing carols on a corner, the light from the street lamps enclosing them in a halo, and a beefy Irish policeman stopped to harmonize with them. There was a jingling music from the bells on the horses as carriages passed by. The light from the shop windows reached out into the street, beating back the darkness like a wave of brilliance.

"So, you are Irish?" the woman said. "I have some relatives there. Where in Ireland do you come from?"

"Ah, well, I've hung my hat in a world of places, ma'am," Peter said. "I'm from all over, really." He did not want to tell an English girl anything about his past. It would be just his luck if she were related to the man he killed.

She marched along like a little sergeant major, and Peter could tell she had a quick mind. Your stories better make sense, boyo, he thought, or she'll sniff out your lying palaver quickly.

He changed the subject, to give him time to think up a past. "But enough about me. Where are you from, if I may ask?"

My family is from Lancashire," she said. "A little town in the countryside. It seems like another world, when I think of how quiet and serene it was. I came here two years ago, when my brother's wife fell ill, but the clamor and the noise and the, the sheer number of *people* here is shocking to me. I have been helping to raise my brother's children, but my heart is back in England."

Then they were at the train depot, a grand brick building with vaulted ceilings and rows of arches, a true temple of progress, of industry. There were people rushing everywhere to get to their trains, and the sound of the steam engines huffing, whistling and clanking was a counterpoint to the buzz of the crowd.

She found the sign for her train, and turned to him, her face ruddy from the cold outside, and said, "You are so kind, but I just realized I do not even know your name, to thank you."

"Francis," he said, surprising himself with how quickly it came out. "James Francis. At your service." He bowed grandly, but he was flushed and nervous, the sweat dripping down his neck underneath his scarf.

"My name is Edith Jones," she said. "And I am pleased to meet you." She did a little curtsey, her green eyes merry and glittering.

He gave her the packages, but, God help him, he could not resist one more thing. He said, "May I see you again, Miss Jones?"

She paused, then smiled and said: "I would like that, Mr. Francis."

"Where do you live?" he said.

"In the town of Merchantville," she said. "But we can meet here in Philadelphia. I ride the train into town every week to buy the ingredients for a good English kidney pie at the market. My brother insists on eating the way he did back in our little village. I will be back next Monday on the 12:00 train. We could meet here if you like. Will you be here?"

"That I will, Miss Jones," Peter said. "That I will."

Walking back from the train station amidst the thronging people, he felt buoyed by the light flooding from the windows, the street lamps, the illuminated signs, the snow -- everywhere he looked it was as bright as day. He felt half mad from the light.

He stopped at a shop window and looked at himself in the reflection. The bright lights made the planes of his face stand out in sharp relief, and he saw for the first time that he had a network of tiny wrinkles at the edges of his eyes. Why, I'm a man in the middle of his years! he thought. He remembered with a pang that in two years he would be forty years old.

Ah, but there was no sense thinking of that on a night like this!

He tipped his hat to the reflection in the glass and went on his way, his spirits lightened by the promise of a new romance.

He did not know how he could manage to be downtown at noontime next Monday, but he knew he must do it, to meet Edith Jones. He must see her again, that was certain.

He realized that next Monday was the Eve of the New Year, the end of the last century and the beginning of a new one.

The dawning of the 1900s! He felt sure that on a day such as that he would be ready to start a new life.

And James Francis was the very name to start it with.

THE END

This is Book One in the series about Rose Sullivan from Skibbereen, Ireland. It is based on some research I did about the Irish women who came to America in the 19th century to work as servants, but the characters are entirely fictional. The ebook version of this book is at: https://www.amazon.com/dp/B00C9JV2R. Links to other books in the series are at the bottom of the page. For other ebook formats, go here: https://www.smashwords.com/books/view/303326.

John McDonnell believes in the power of imagination and language to transform life. He has done many types of writing, but fiction is closest to his heart. He writes in the horror, sci-fi, romance, humor and fantasy genres. He lives near Philadelphia, Pennsylvania with his wife and four children.

Visit my Website for news about my upcoming projects. It's at http://www.johnfmcdonnell.com.

Did you like this book? Send me an email: mailto:mcdonnellwrite@gmail.com

Connect with me on Facebook! I'm at https://www.facebook.com/john.mcdonnell2.

Made in the USA
Coppell, TX
14 June 2020

28114503R00075